Hearing Voices

By the same author

So Far From Skye
Jess and the River Kids
Stringybark Summer
Deepwater
The Message

Judith O'Neill

Hearing Voices

Hamish Hamilton · London

HAMISH HAMILTON LTD

Published by the Penguin Group
Penguin Books Ltd, 27 Wrights Lane, London W8 5TZ, England
Penguin Books USA Inc., 375 Hudson Street, New York, New York 10014, USA
Penguin Books Australia Ltd, Ringwood, Victoria, Australia
Penguin Books Canada Ltd, 10 Alcorn Avenue, Toronto, Ontario, Canada M4V 3B2
Penguin Books (NZ) Ltd, 182–190 Wairau Road, Auckland 10, New Zealand

Penguin Books Ltd, Registered Offices: Harmondsworth, Middlesex, England

First published 1996
1 3 5 7 9 10 8 6 4 2

Typeset in Bembo by
Rowland Phototypesetting Ltd,
Bury St Edmunds, Suffolk

Made and printed in Great Britain by
Clays Ltd, St Ives plc

A CIP catalogue record for this book is available from the British Library

ISBN 0-241-13674-1

For my cousin Heather Vines
and for all her grandchildren
and in loving memory of Geoffrey Vines

Contents

1

Coming Home from School

Edinburgh, Scotland

Walking home from Gillespie's High School with Fiona on that windy autumn afternoon, Malcolm was trying to sort out his oddly mixed feelings about the trip to Australia.

'It's not exactly that I don't *want* to go,' he said hesitantly, keeping his eyes fixed on the grass as they crossed the Meadows. Yellow leaves were whirling off the trees and blowing against their faces. 'I'd really like to see the country where Dad and Mum grew up. I've been hearing about the place ever since I was born! You'd think Australia was some kind of heaven on earth from the way they talk about it.'

'Then what's the problem?' Fiona asked him. She smiled. He lifted his eyes towards hers for a fleeting minute but then turned them back to the grass. He felt safer that way.

'It'd be all right if I was just going to meet Dad's brother and his two sisters and their children,' he said. 'I could manage that. They're my close family. I've seen their photos. I know their names. But this thing I have to go to in Geelong is an absolutely *huge* gathering. There'll be *hundreds* of people there, Fiona! All of them descended

I

from my great-great-grandparents. Or maybe it's my great-great-great-grandparents. Dad keeps telling me but I can never remember.'

Fiona laughed.

'I've never even *heard* of my great-great-great-grandparents,' she said. 'I don't think I ever had any!'

'Everyone's got them!' Malcolm said, joining in her easy laughter. 'But Scots aren't so obsessed with them as Australians are. That's the difference!'

'Have they hired a big hall or something? They'll never fit those hundreds of relations into your uncle's house, will they?'

'There's not just a hall! There's a whole park and a whole football field! And this MacDonald family gathering lasts for a whole weekend! There's going to be a picnic and a dance and a church service and a visit to some mouldy old house. People are coming from all over Australia.'

'A dance!' Fiona exclaimed. 'That'll be fun. I could easily give the church service a miss but I wish I could be at the dance!'

'*I* wish you could too!' Malcolm burst out before he could stop himself. He wondered if he had gone too far. He glanced at Fiona. She didn't seem to mind. In fact she was looking quite pleased. Neither of them spoke for a while.

'I think I can understand why you feel a bit scared,' Fiona said at last. 'I wouldn't want to meet such an enormous crowd of people myself. Whatever could I say to so many?'

'Yes! That's exactly it,' Malcolm said in relief. 'I'm sure I'll get tongue-tied or start stammering the way I sometimes do when Mr Murray asks me to stand up in class and speak. I'll just open my mouth and no words'll come out. It won't be easy, like talking to you.'

Fiona laughed comfortably. She flicked back her long brown hair, hitched her bag higher up her shoulder and looked at him with calm grey eyes.

'You know what your dad's always saying, Malcolm,' she said. '"Blood's thicker than water." When you come face to face with those hundreds of relations, perhaps you'll feel as if you've always known them. You probably even *look* like them! I bet they've all got straight black hair like yours and brown eyes and that same funny dimple in one cheek. You probably won't have to say much. You'll only have to nod and smile and let them do the talking. They'll like that.'

'I just wish you were coming with me, Fiona!' The words sprang out of his mouth more loudly than he'd intended. His cheeks were burning though he hoped they weren't.

'I wish I could come too,' said Fiona. 'I want to get to the bottom of the whole mystery of why your parents packed up and left Australia two years before you were born. Sixteen years they've been living here in Scotland and never been back once! Not even for a funeral! It's very odd.'

'There's no mystery!' said Malcolm indignantly. 'Dad just wanted a change of scene. That's what he always says.'

'I know that's what he *says*, Malcolm, but it's very peculiar. There he was, a successful lawyer in Melbourne. An advocate. What's that word they use for an advocate out there?'

'Barrister. Same as in England.'

'That's it. He was a brilliant barrister, or so he tells you. Rolling in money, probably. Suddenly he throws it all up and moves to Scotland and changes to teaching history in a high school. It's mad!'

'But he couldn't go on being a lawyer here, could he?'

3

Malcolm said quickly. 'Scottish law's different. Luckily he'd studied history as well as law in Melbourne so he just had to do one year here in Edinburgh to train as a teacher. And he really loves it now. He says he's much happier teaching history than being a barrister. Less hassle, he says.'

'I still think it's strange. You'll have to ask your uncle and your aunts about it. Your dad's definitely trying to hide something. Probably there was some huge family row. A quarrel over your granny's will maybe.'

Malcolm couldn't help laughing out loud at her wild theories. His voice broke unexpectedly in the middle of his laugh and then came back to rest in its usual place. 'I don't think so, Fiona, honestly. Dad gets on so well with his brother and his sisters. Writes them letters every month and phones them for their birthdays. He wouldn't do that if there'd been a quarrel, would he? He really *wants* me to be there for this big family gathering. He'd go himself if he could get away.'

'But look how your dad's still obsessed with the law,' said Fiona. 'Look how he reads up all the cases in the newspaper every week. Look how he wants *you* to do law yourself!'

Malcolm sighed. She was right about that. Dad was always trying to push him into the idea of studying law when he'd finished school. Dad never seemed to listen when he said he really wanted to be a vet.

'Would you l-like to c-come up to our f-flat for a while?' The stammer that sometimes struck Malcolm in the middle of Mr Murray's lessons had come back again. He pressed on more quickly and pretended not to notice. 'My m-mum'd be p-pleased to see you. You c-could have tea with us. You c-could phone your m-mother and t-tell her you'll b-be a b-bit late home. It's my l-last chance to s-see you.'

'Thanks, I'd like to,' she said and he felt the stammer disappear at once as if he had swallowed it. Fiona was pleased he'd asked her to come up for tea before she'd even reached her own front door. She knew he often wanted to ask but sometimes he just couldn't find the right words. He seemed to lose his voice at the last minute.

'I've got a present for you,' said Fiona suddenly as the two of them climbed the grey stone stairs to the Mac-Donalds' top flat. She was scrabbling about in her bag for a thin brown parcel as long as a school ruler.

'What is it?' Malcolm's dark eyes were suddenly full of surprise and delight. He hadn't expected a present.

'Open it on the plane,' said Fiona, smiling up at him. 'It's more Irish than Scottish really but once you get the hang of it I think you'll like it. It's just for fun. Bring it safely back with you! And don't forget me, whatever happens!'

'Never!' breathed Malcolm, looking her full in the face as they reached the top landing, crowded with Mum's green plants.

The Mallee, Victoria, Australia

On that same Friday afternoon, far away in Australia, Eileen Gallagher had come to the end of another school day, another school week. All the country buses were lined up outside Ouyen Secondary College as Eileen climbed on to her own bus for Torrita to the west and then for the farms further north. Her older brother Kevin wasn't coming home this weekend. He was staying on in Ouyen at his friend Jim's place. They had a match to play on Saturday and a barbecue on Sunday.

At Galah and Walpeup and at farm gates along the Mallee Highway, schoolkids were set down to trudge their last lap home or to leap into a mother's waiting car or to jump on to their own old motorbikes, hidden safely all day in the scrub. At Torrita the bus turned north on to a rougher, narrower road. A few more halts to let off the last of her friends and then Eileen was alone on the bus. She quite liked that. Her stop was at the very end of the run, up towards the Pink Lakes and Yanga-Nyawi, on the edge of the Sunset Country.

From her seat at the back of the bus, Eileen stared out at the red Mallee earth and the strip of wild scrubland bursting into brilliant spring flowers between the roadway and the fence. Slowly, without quite meaning to, she closed her eyes. She wasn't going to sleep. Nothing like that. She was just thinking. Thinking about the big family gathering at the end of next week, down south in Geelong. Who'd be there? she wondered. Nice Aunty Helen, perhaps? Those irritating city cousins? And wasn't some boy flying out from Scotland? She'd ask Mum more about it tonight. Mum was the one who was so excited about this gathering. She'd even persuaded the schools to let Kevin and Eileen and little Jack have a whole week off from Wednesday. She'd told the teachers it would be educational. Eileen wondered.

Suddenly she opened her eyes again. Something was oddly different. She wasn't quite alone on the bus after all. A girl was sitting there, right beside her. The driver's kid, perhaps? Eileen had certainly never seen her before. An old-fashioned sort of girl in a plain dark dress with long sleeves and a white scarf knotted around her neck. Her hair was parted in the middle and pushed back behind her ears. She seemed about the same age as Eileen but smaller. A nice enough face. Quite a serious face really, for a girl of thirteen, but smiling pleasantly all the same and gazing out at the flowering Mallee.

Now the girl's eyes sparkled with delight. An emu was scuttling along beside the bus, brown feathers ruffled, neck stretched out, legs moving fast, keeping pace with the wheels. The girl leapt up in excitement, leaning her forehead against the cool glass of the window and staring in fascination at the racing emu. Eileen glanced down at the girl's feet. They were completely bare! Bare dirty feet! On the school bus! It was unusual, to say the least. Eileen looked up sideways. The girl seemed quite at ease, not worried about her filthy feet, but smiling, always smiling at the emu.

At that moment Eileen caught the faint and tantalizing scent of aniseed or something very like aniseed. Was that strange girl wolfing down a whole bagful of aniseed balls? In an instant Eileen decided to ask her for one. That wouldn't be rude. In fact it was very rude of the girl to be eating aniseed balls without offering her any. She turned abruptly to face her and held out an open hand.

But the girl wasn't there! The bus was empty again, apart from the silent driver. Only the scent of something like aniseed still lingered in the air. Eileen shivered and blinked her eyes. She moved quickly up the lurching bus to be nearer the driver. She talked at him, loudly and cheerfully, about the family trip down south next week, until the moment when he slammed on his brakes right outside the Gallaghers' farm gate.

'There you are, kid!' he said with a cheery grin as she climbed down. 'Home at last! Say g'day to your mum and dad for me. See you Mondee.'

'I must have dreamt it all,' Eileen murmured to herself as she walked up the soft red track to the house.

2

Letters from Morag

As the plane lifted off from Heathrow, Malcolm stretched his legs right out into the aisle. The seats were cramped and too close together. Between him and the window sat an elderly Australian couple, going home after their trip to Britain. They were sorting through a box of colour slides, slotting each one into their viewer, passing it from hand to hand and laughing out loud as they recalled their wet day at Stratford-upon-Avon or their misty day at Windermere. Malcolm began to feel irritated by them already. Were they going to keep up this noisy chuckling the whole way to Melbourne?

He closed his eyes and let his mind go back to last night at home in Edinburgh. It had been a mistake to tell Dad he was feeling a bit scared of meeting the Australian relations.

'Blood's thicker than water, son,' Dad had said, half smiling at him but impatient too. 'You'll like them the minute you meet them.'

Malcolm had shaken his head. Dad was suddenly exasperated.

'You don't seem to care a scrap about our family!' he'd said. 'This is a wonderful opportunity I'm giving you, and your school's very generous to let you go off for two weeks in the middle of term.'

'I know all that, Dad,' Malcolm had said quickly. 'I'm glad to be going. I really do want to see the bush and the kangaroos and the hot sandy beaches you and Mum are always talking about. But just think of those hundreds of first cousins and second cousins and third cousins I've never even met before! Australia's a foreign country to me. Scotland's my real home.'

Dad had looked shocked and hurt. Australia was still as fresh in his mind as if he'd left it only yesterday. But Malcolm was right, of course. He'd never been there. All he knew were the prints of famous Australian paintings hanging on the walls of their high Edinburgh flat, the tea-towels covered with pictures of wallabies and wombats in their kitchen, and the wads of photographs that arrived every Christmas from Dad's brother in Geelong and Mum's sister in Bendigo. Photographs of cousins and still more cousins, all looking strangely familiar and yet unfamiliar, gathered around countless barbecues under brilliant blue skies. Malcolm had never examined those cousins' faces very closely. He had always been much more interested in the extraordinary weather.

'Sorry, Dad,' Malcolm had said, seeing the pain in his father's face. 'I didn't mean to say "foreign country". I just meant "unknown country". I'm sure I'll love the *place* but I'm not quite sure if I'll love those hordes of relations.'

'The rellies!' his father had said with a grin, slipping into the affectionate Australian word.

'Yes, the rellies. Like this Uncle Don who's going to collect me at the airport. Your "little brother" as you always call him, though he must be well over forty by now.'

'You don't need to be scared of meeting Don! He's the nicest of the lot. My older sisters are a bit bossy, I have to admit, but you'll like them too once you know them.

I only wish your grandparents were still alive to see you!'

As the plane flew high over Europe, Malcolm bent down to his bag and took out Fiona's thin parcel. He couldn't wait to undo her careful knots so he pulled off the string and brown paper in one go. The present fell out and Malcolm laughed. It was a tin whistle, a penny whistle as the label said, with six stops and a blue mouthpiece. He had no idea how to play the thing. Forgetting where he was, he put the mouthpiece between his lips, covered three of the holes with his fingers and blew hard. A piercing silvery note rang out. The couple beside him jumped in fright. They stared at him.

'S-sorry,' he murmured, red in the face, and pushed the whistle down into the pocket of his jeans.

He bent to his bag again. This time he pulled out a large padded envelope and tipped its contents on to his knees. These were the precious family documents Dad wanted him to take to the gathering in Australia. First, the old photograph of a black house on the Isle of Skye. Low stone walls, a ragged turf roof, no chimney, a shaggy Highland cow being milked by the front door. Malcolm knew this wasn't exactly the home of his ancestors. *That* poor little hut near Talisker must have fallen down long ago. This was simply a typical black house that had somehow survived on Skye until 1939 when the photograph had been taken. Dad said it would give everyone in the family a good idea of the kind of home Donald and Effie MacDonald had left behind them when they and their children had sailed away from the misty island in 1852. Malcolm slid the photograph back into its envelope.

What he really wanted was another look at those letters. Not the *original* letters, of course. They were still in the National Library of Scotland where Dad had discovered them only last month. They couldn't be removed but Dad had had these photocopies made. They certainly looked the real thing. Every stain and crease from the faded old papers in the library had been faithfully reproduced.

The first three letters were in Gaelic. Malcolm couldn't understand a word of them so he flicked through the pages until he came to the English translations Dad had pinned at the back. These letters were written by one of the children of Donald and Effie MacDonald. Her name was Morag, she seemed to be about thirteen years old, and she was writing to the Free Church minister at Carbost on the Isle of Skye. She'd written the first letter from a sailing ship, the *Georgiana*, somewhere out in the Atlantic on the long voyage to the new colony of Victoria in Australia. The second came from the same ship, at anchor near Geelong, just as Morag and her family were about to disembark and go to work on a distant sheep-run. She spoke of a terrible mutiny on board. Malcolm had often heard his father talk about that mutiny. It was part of his family's history, passed down from father to son.

The third letter was written from a log hut on the sheep-run itself, a place called Brolga Marsh. Morag said that Brolga Marsh was almost as big as Skye itself. Malcolm found that hard to believe. She seemed to like the new country all right though she found everything very strange. She was asking the minister to persuade more of the poor crofters on Skye to follow them out there. *They will never be hungry again*, she wrote but she did admit that her mother was sometimes desperately homesick. That was about all. Morag seemed very fond of her older brother, Allan, and she spoke about two other boys from the ship – Rory MacRae and Jimmy MacLean. Malcolm couldn't tell if she really liked either of the boys or which one she liked better. That was the whole trouble with Morag

MacDonald. She never said enough. He wished she'd said more.

Now he turned to the fourth letter. This one was quite different. It was written in English for one thing and it was dated 1874. Morag was no longer a girl of thirteen but a woman of well over thirty, living on a small farm at the foot of Mount Macedon. She was still writing to the same minister, Mr Cameron. He must have been an old man by this time. Morag was married to Rory MacRae (so she *had* eventually decided which boy she liked better!) and they already had several children. It was a terrible letter. Malcolm could hardly bear to read the words. It was all about her brother Allan. Allan MacDonald had disappeared! He was probably dead, Morag wrote bitterly, but no one knew for certain.

She told the minister first how Allan had married Kirsty Nicolson. *You'll remember her well, Mr Cameron. She used to be Kirsty Gordon and she lived with her mother and brothers in a quarry on Skye until they came with us to the ship.* Allan and Kirsty had gone to live in Adelaide, hundreds of miles away, soon after their marriage. He had found a good steady job. They'd had six lovely children – Allan, Neil, Calum, Morag, Kenneth and Gordon. Suddenly, quite out of the blue, Allan had written to Morag to tell her he was going off to join some expedition that was trying to cross the vast desert from Alice Springs to Perth in Western Australia. Kirsty had begged him not to go, he'd said, but he was going all the same. Morag herself had written at once to tell him he'd be mad to leave his young family. He might not be back for a year or more. What would become of them? But Allan insisted that he'd worked hard and saved carefully. He was leaving Kirsty plenty of money to feed and clothe the family for at least a year. The neighbours would keep a friendly eye on her. He'd be safely home again well before the year was up. Allan said he simply *had* to go. He'd always dreamt of exploring the mysterious red centre of their new country. He'd been chosen by the expedition's leader out of hundreds of men who wanted to go. He couldn't miss this chance of a lifetime. No harm could possibly come to him, he said.

But harm *had* come, wrote Morag in despair. After fifteen months, six members of the expedition had staggered, naked and exhausted, into a coastal township hundreds of miles north of Perth. They'd nearly starved to death. They'd had to eat their camels. They'd had to dig in the sand for water every day and they'd licked it up desperately, drop by drop. They were bitten all over by savage ants and burnt by the sun. Worst of all, Allan was no longer with them! The leader said that one night Allan had gone right out of his mind with hunger and thirst and had wandered away from their camp in the desert. They'd called and searched with what little strength they had left but they'd never found him. He'd gone for good. He must be dead. No white man could survive alone among those sandhills. No one could live without water. Morag poured out her heart to the old minister at Carbost.

You remember how I always loved my brother, Mr Cameron, she said, *and now I'll never see him again. Poor Kirsty had to put her six children into the orphanage for a few months but now she has found a position as housekeeper to a widower with three young children at Penola. The man is willing to take her children too. I am very angry with Allan, even though he is dead! He never should have gone off on that expedition! My mother and father are heart-broken. They often speak of you, Mr Cameron, and they wish you were here in the Colony to comfort and advise them. If only we had stayed on Skye, such a terrible thing would never have happened.*

Malcolm folded up the letter and tried to remember

just how he was connected to this Morag woman. There was something he quite liked about her. He almost seemed to hear her sad, strong voice in his ears. He fished out the family tree his father had drawn up for him. There at the top were the ancestors, Donald and Effie MacDonald from the Isle of Skye, and there were the four children: Allan, Morag, Flora and Kenny. On the right-hand side Dad had written in the name of a baby cousin, Katie, who'd been found in Greenock in 1852 and somehow taken along with them on to the ship. Malcolm ran his finger down the lines from Morag's children, full of hope. No. He wasn't descended from her though she seemed to have an awful lot of great-great-great-grandchildren. Would they all be at the gathering? He tried Allan's line next. Yes, that was the one. Malcolm wasn't entirely happy to be descended from a madman who'd left his family and gone off into the desert and completely disappeared. He wished he belonged to Morag or even to Flora or Kenny or that poor little cousin, Katie. They seemed much more sensible. The only good thing to be said for Allan was that he did have a sense of adventure. But look where it had led him!

Malcolm pressed his hands over his ears to block out the conversation of the couple next to him on the plane. Abruptly, the woman pushed her colour slides back into their box and leant her head of tight curls against Malcolm's shoulder. Without even asking him if he minded, she fell asleep. She slept till the steward brought round the first of many meals on a plastic tray. As he ate the food with his plastic knife and fork, Malcolm thought about Morag MacDonald's three-month voyage to Australia in a sailing ship. Which would be worse? he wondered. That crowded *Georgiana*, slowly dipping its way across the ocean, or this jumbo jet with its closely packed rows of bodies, hurtling the passengers to Melbourne in twenty-three hours. He thought he'd prefer the ship, in spite of the creaking timbers and the terrible seasickness. He would have had time to make friends on a ship. Morag had written about singing and dancing and story-telling on board. It sounded quite good fun.

The blinds were drawn down now to blot out the long night. Malcolm clamped on a pair of headphones and watched a film about a dog. The huddled passengers slept or snoozed or laughed out loud at the film. He had never known time to pass so slowly. At Singapore, the Australian couple left the plane for a two-day stopover. Malcolm spent an hour walking briskly up and down the wide concourse at the airport, trying to get the circulation going in his legs, gazing at the glittering array of perfumes and jewellery, listening to the fountain splashing in its pool. He couldn't quite believe he was actually there, on the edge of Asia. He bought a postcard and an airmail stamp and wrote to Fiona back in Edinburgh.

I'm more than halfway there. Missing you. Thanks for the penny whistle. Don't forget me.
Love, Malcolm.

He posted his card and hurried back to the plane. This time no one was sitting beside him. He put up the armrests and lay down with a pillow under his head and a blanket over his back. When he woke he eased the blind up a few centimetres. It was still night out there. He stared at the blazing Australian stars above and at the shadowy continent far below. Was that the desert where Allan MacDonald had disappeared so long ago?

On Tuesday, the plane landed at Melbourne just as the sun was rising. Malcolm joined a shuffling queue for passport control and then collected his luggage from the carousel. He walked slowly towards the exit. This was the moment he'd been dreading. Somehow he had to find his Uncle Don out there. He stepped through the doorway and faced a crowd of eager faces peering over the barrier. Some people held large notices high in their hands to catch the passengers' attention. *Welcome home, Grandma! Mr John Robertson of Outdoor Adventures Pty Ltd.* Malcolm searched in vain for a notice saying *MacDonald.* He wished now that he'd looked a bit more closely at those family photographs last Christmas.

'That must be him, Mum!' shrieked a tall, red-haired girl in the very front of the crowd. 'That boy by himself. The one with the pale face and the dark hair. He's exactly like the photo his dad sent us. Hi, Malkie! We're here!'

Malcolm looked at the girl.

'Do you mean me?' he said in surprise. No one had ever called him Malkie before.

'Are you Malcolm MacDonald?' the girl's mother asked, leaning over the barrier and smiling. She reached out one hand to touch him.

He nodded.

'I knew it!' cried the girl, her green eyes full of light. 'Come on, Malkie! I'm Chloë! Your long-lost cousin!' She ducked under the railing and shot out her arm to take his case.

'I can manage it,' he said.

'Give it to me, Malcolm,' said the girl's father, beaming down at him. 'Welcome home to the family! We're going to give you a great time.'

So this bouncy, cheerful, balding man was Dad's little brother! Uncle Don! He'd always been wearing a broad-brimmed hat in the photos. The smooth dome of his bald head made him look quite different. Malcolm followed the three of them out to the car park where a dawn chorus of birds was chirping away loudly in the strangely drab trees. The red-haired cousin walked along with a self-confident swing, humming a song to herself. The friendly Australian voices of these three MacDonalds were slow and relaxed as if they had all the time in the world.

Uncle Don's car was huge and silent. As it skimmed down the almost-empty freeway, Aunty Jan unhooked the phone and rang straight through to Malcolm's father in Edinburgh.

'He's here!' she shouted, as if her voice had to reach across oceans by its own efforts. 'Safe and sound. No worries.' She passed the phone to Malcolm in the back seat.

'Yes, everything's f-fine, Dad,' he muttered, embarrassed at being overheard. 'I had a good sleep on the p-plane. N-no, we're not at the house yet. We're in the c-car, zooming down the Geelong road. Yes, in the c-car! It's only s-six in the morning and everything's quiet. Yes. I'll remember. Give my love to Mum. And to F-F-Fiona too, if you s-see her. Bye, Dad.'

'Who's Fiona?' Chloë demanded at once.

'Just a f-friend from school,' Malcolm mumbled, his cheeks flushing.

Chloë laughed.

Malcolm was astonished by his uncle's large modern house, set in a garden full of trees. Every house in the street was different and stood a long way from its neighbours. There was no fence along the front and none at the sides. No hedge or gate. No footpath or pavement beside the road either. Wherever did they walk when they had to dash to the local corner shop for a pint of milk? Did they tramp along the green lawn by the gutter's edge? Did they walk right on the roadway where any car might hit them? The flowering bushes were dripping from rain that had fallen in the night. The yellow wattle trees were blazing. Birds were whistling and calling. Everything smelt fresh and clean. Even the air seemed different from the Edinburgh air. Malcolm felt slightly drunk with the excitement of breathing the extraordinary stuff in and out of his lungs. Australia really was another world.

'Breakfast first,' Aunty Jan said as they walked in through the back door. 'The main gathering doesn't start till Saturday, Malcolm, so you'll have time to get over the jet lag. We're meeting up with some distant cousins called Woodburn on Friday. Chloë, just show Malcolm where he's going to sleep.'

Chloë pushed open a door. Sunshine was streaming in through the large windows.

'This is Harry's room,' she said. 'You can have it while you're here.'

'Where's Harry?' Malcolm asked her, disappointed. He'd been almost looking forward to meeting his cousin Harry.

'Uni. Brisbane,' Chloë said.

'Brisbane! In Queensland! That's a long way to go to university!'

'Harry says the further the better.'

'Won't he be coming back for the family gathering?'

Chloë shook her head. 'Harry's not so keen on family,' she said.

Malcolm liked the sound of this Harry even more.

'I love your accent, Malkie,' Chloë said suddenly.

Malcolm bridled. 'I haven't got an accent!' he said indignantly. 'I just talk normally. Like everyone else.'

'It may sound normal to you but it sounds very Scottish to me. I love it! It's really sweet the way you roll your r's. And the funny way you say "gathering".'

'Gathering, gathering,' Malcolm repeated silently. It didn't sound funny at all.

Chloë left him. He opened his case and hunted out the tin of shortbread for his aunt and the bottle of Talisker whisky for his uncle. He picked up the padded envelope and carried everything through to the kitchen.

'And the letters, Malcolm?' Uncle Don asked, hugging the whisky bottle delightedly to his chest. 'Did you bring those letters from Morag? The ones your father found in the library?'

Malcolm handed over the envelope. His uncle grasped it. 'She was an amazing woman, that Morag. A real pioneer. What I like most about her was that she was always so fond of our old Allan. That's what all the family stories say, anyway. And she had the second sight, my grandfather told me. She could see things far ahead, long before they happened, and she could talk with ghosts from the past. Just occasionally she'd have a strange compulsion to go quickly to some particular place and, when she got there, someone always needed her help. An amazing woman!'

'She didn't exactly see that our old Allan was going to disappear,' said Malcolm bluntly. 'Though she did warn him not to go.'

'Disappear?' exclaimed Uncle Don in astonishment.

'It's in one of the letters. Dad had never heard about it either. I think the family must've kept quiet about it. A bit embarrassing really, to have an ancestor who disappears.'

Chloë and her father made a grab for the letters and read them quickly, one by one.

'It's terrible!' cried Uncle Don, his face white with indignation, at the end of Morag's last letter. 'Why weren't we told?'

'Never mind about all that old history, whatever it is,' said Aunty Jan briskly, giving Malcolm a sudden hug as she sat him down to a good breakfast. 'When you've been in Australia for two weeks, Mal, you'll wonder why your father ever left it.'

'As a matter of fact, Aunty, I *do* wonder why he left it!' Malcolm said, remembering Fiona's theory about a family quarrel. 'Do *you* know why?'

For a long silent minute Malcolm was sure Aunty Jan was going to tell him something. Then she seemed to change her mind.

'You've got that MacDonald dimple!' she said with a laugh. 'Just like your grandfather's. He was a lovely man!'

Malcolm rubbed his cheek.

'Mum, the airletter!' Chloë cried. 'We've forgotten to give him the airletter! Where did you put it?'

'On top of the fridge, dear.'

Chloë leapt up and found the flimsy blue airletter. She held it towards Malcolm with a grin.

'How could it get here so soon?' he asked her in amazement, reaching out his hand.

'She must have written it a week before you left.'

'Who? Is it from Mum?' His mind was racing.

'No!' said Chloë. 'It's from someone called Ms F. J. Douglas. Her name's on the back.'

'Oh!' gasped Malcolm, tearing open the airletter. 'That's Fiona!'

'Just a friend from school?' Chloë asked with a laugh. Aunty Jan and Uncle Don were smiling down at him.

3

Heirlooms

Early on Wednesday morning, the Gallaghers were loading up their car at the farm. Red sand whipped against their faces and a red October sun was already warming their backs. Eileen's father had climbed right on top of the car. He was roping the foot-plough to the roof-rack.

'Hey, Dad! Do we really have to take that ridiculous thing?' Eileen called up to him with a laugh. Her straight fair hair, cut short, lifted in the wind. Now that the moment had come to leave, she felt her excitement rising.

'Of course we do, Eileen. You read the letter yourself, didn't you? *Bring any heirlooms and mementoes*, it said. This is our only heirloom so we're taking it. If your mother's ancestors managed to lug this plough the whole way from Scotland to Australia, surely we can take it a few hundred kilometres from here to Geelong. There! That's good and tight. Let's be off. We'll be all day on the road so I want to get started.'

Dad jumped to the ground in one flying leap. Mum was in the car already. Eileen climbed into the back seat with Kevin and Jack. Piled up behind were the sleeping-bags and the tents and all the rest of their camping gear. Eileen hopped out to open and close every gate till they'd left the farm behind. At Torrita they turned east to Ouyen and then south on to the Sunraysia Highway.

'Mum, who exactly is this guy Rex Woodburn?' Eileen asked as they sped south through the Mallee sandhills. 'The one who wrote to you. Do we know him?'

'Never heard of him till his letter came, dear,' her mother said, turning round to smile at Eileen. 'He says he's descended from Flora MacDonald just as we're descended from Morag. There were two other children in the original family and a poor little orphan cousin they picked up on the way. I expect this Rex Woodburn has tracked down lots of their descendants too. I just happened to see that advertisement he put in the Melbourne news-paper back in March so I wrote and said we'd like to come to this gathering he's organizing. He tells me he put the same notice in the main papers all over Australia. He's had answers from everywhere, he says.'

'So how many people will be there?' Eileen asked, delighted at the prospect of such a crop of unknown cousins.

'Could be hundreds,' said Dad.

'Thousands!' said Kev. 'Those early settlers had huge families. Look at our old Morag. That ancestor of yours, Mum. Didn't she have eleven children?'

'I just don't know how she managed to look after so many!' Mum said. 'You three are more than enough for me. Morag must've been worn out, poor woman.'

'Lots of children died young in those days,' Jack piped up cheerfully.

'Only two of Morag's died young,' said Mum. 'That still left her with nine and most of them had ten or more children of their own. She must've had at least eighty grandchildren!'

'So Morag is my great-great-grandmother?' Eileen asked.

'No, I think she's your great-great-great-grandmother. It's hard to keep track of all those generations.'

'I bet we won't have much in common with those hundreds of other people at the gathering,' Kev said, doing some calculations in his head. 'The MacDonald genes must be watered down after all this time. If Morag is our great-great-great, then we've only got one thirty-second bit of her in our veins.'

'Hardly seems worth this long trek south just for a little scrap of a gene like that,' said Dad, pretending to be bored with the whole thing.

'Denis!' exclaimed Mum. 'It'll be *well* worth it! Blood's thicker than water. We're sure to find someone congenial in all that crowd. Anyway, we'll be seeing the cousins we know already. And there's that boy flying all the way out from Scotland to join the gathering. I want to make sure we meet *him*.'

'Why ever does he live in Scotland?' asked Eileen in genuine surprise. 'Did his ancestor get left behind when the ship sailed?'

'No,' laughed Mum. 'Rex Woodburn tells me his parents moved there about sixteen years ago. Before this boy was born. Some trouble in his dad's law firm, I think.'

'I bet his dad embezzled the funds!' cried Kev in delight. 'He had to flee!'

'No, no, nothing like that,' said Mum, shocked at the very thought. 'He probably didn't quite see eye to eye with the senior partner. It's a MacDonald family failing.'

Dad nodded and laughed. 'If that boy's father had been suspected of embezzling anything, Kev,' he said, 'he would have been brought straight back to stand trial here. You can't escape the law just by moving to Scotland.'

Kevin gave up his theory reluctantly. He rather liked the idea of an embezzler in the family.

'The only peculiar thing about that letter from Rex Woodburn,' Mum went on, 'was what he said about the castle. He seems to have the idea that our ancestors came from a *castle* on the Isle of Skye. He says he's been back there on a trip and he thinks he's found it – or the ruins of it, anyway. He's even got a photo to show us.'

'But, Mum, they *didn't* come from a castle!' Eileen protested, laughing.

'No, they certainly didn't. The poor things lived in some kind of hut. A black house, they called it. Nothing but a stone shack with a turf roof. The cow used to spend the winter in there with them. My grandmother had so many stories about that hut. She'd heard them from *her* grandmother, I suppose. Our family was just like all the other emigrants from Skye on the *Georgiana*. They were dirt poor. They had nothing but the rags they stood up in.'

'And the foot-plough,' said Dad, rolling his eyes towards the roof of the car.

'I bet they had a Bible,' said Eileen. 'People in the olden days always had Bibles.'

'I wonder what's become of it?' said Mum, frowning. 'I've never seen it.'

'Probably Allan got it,' said Dad. 'Didn't you say the eldest brother was called Allan?'

'But it's odd he didn't get the plough, Denis. You'd think the eldest son would get the plough. The eldest *daughter* should've had the Bible.'

'We'll never know how they divided up the things, Mum,' said Eileen. 'It's too far back. But I'm sure we'll see that Bible at the gathering on Saturday. Someone will be waving it proudly in the air.'

'It'll be a Gaelic Bible, probably,' said Mum. 'That was the language they spoke, you know. They had to start learning English on the ship.'

The day was long. The stops for food and hot tea and a change of driver became more frequent. The irritations in the back seat grew worse. But late in the evening they came at last to the camping ground at Ocean Grove, right by the mouth of the Barwon River. They pitched their tents in the dark and crawled into their sleeping-bags.

The next morning the whole family sat outside in the sunshine, eating pancakes for breakfast. Dad himself was making them in a flat pan over the barbecue. He tossed each one with an expert flick of his wrist. Eileen was gazing around at all the colourful tents and caravans.

'Didn't Rex Woodburn say some other relations of ours might be camping here, Mum?' she asked. 'Who are they?'

'An elderly couple called MacRae. They must be Morag's people too, just like us. Morag married a MacRae, remember. They're bringing their caravan over from Tasmania. Rex seems to know everyone's travelling plans. He's got us all listed on his computer!'

'Let's try to find the MacRaes,' said Kev, jumping up.

'Spot the rellies!' squeaked Jack.

'Come on, then,' said Eileen, swallowing her last mouthful of pancake. 'This is a good time. Everyone's eating outside.'

'Don't stare!' Mum warned them, settling back into her chair. 'It's rude.'

There were many elderly couples with caravans on the camp-ground. They all looked much alike. Grey-haired, spry and cheerful. Only the caravans were different, some ancient and battered, some new and luxurious.

'We'd better find a Tassy number-plate,' said Jack. 'It's not really rude to stare at number-plates.'

'There's one!' said Eileen. 'That big red and white van on the left.'

'And there's another!' Kev shouted, pointing to the very last caravan by the river's edge.

Each of the Tasmanian caravans had an elderly couple sitting outside it.

'I'm going to ask this lot,' Eileen said, turning towards the red and white one.

'You can't!' protested Jack.

'Watch me!' she said.

Eileen tossed back her pale hair and strode confidently towards the old couple who sat placidly in the sunshine, sipping their tea and reading their newspapers.

'Excuse me,' she said.

The couple looked up, surprised. Eileen took a deep breath. 'You're not going to the MacDonald family gathering on Saturday, are you? At Queen's Park in Geelong?'

The man shook his head.

'Nope,' he said pleasantly. 'Just on holiday, love. Getting right away from our family, as a matter of fact.'

'Sorry,' mumbled Eileen and hurried back to the boys. The scattering of small freckles stood out clearly on her nose and forehead, the way they always did when she was embarrassed.

The old caravan by the water's edge needed a coat of paint. This elderly couple were small. Their faces were brown and gnarled from years under the sun. Like retired gnomes, thought Eileen.

'Excuse me,' she said, approaching the small man and smiling at him.

The man stared at her in astonishment.

'Just look at that girl, Gill!' he gasped. 'That girl with the fair hair! She's the image of our Anna!'

Now the woman was staring. There were tears in her eyes.

'Anna!' she cried, leaping up and holding out both her arms to Eileen.

'S-sorry,' Eileen stammered, taking a step backwards. 'I'm not Anna. I'm Eileen. We just wondered if you were on your way to the same family gathering as us. The MacDonald gathering on Saturday.'

The old woman sank into her chair again and rubbed her eyes.

'Yes, we are,' she said, trying to hide her disappointment.

'You look so like our poor Anna, you see,' said the man, grasping his wife's hand to comfort her. 'Our granddaughter. You gave us a bit of a shock, that's all. Our Anna was just about your age. Same hair. Same eyes. Same freckles.'

'Same lovely smile,' said his wife, her voice shaking.

Eileen felt strange. Not quite herself.

'Is your poor Anna coming to the family gathering?' Jack blurted out.

'No,' said the man.

There was an awkward pause. Then the man spoke again. His voice sounded thick. 'Anna died. A year ago, it was. We miss her.'

Eileen didn't know what to say. Before she could find any words, Kev had butted in. 'We're descended from Morag MacDonald,' he said proudly.

'So are we!' the man exclaimed in delight, pushing away his sadness. 'Which of her children do you come from?'

'Effie,' said Eileen who'd heard it often enough. 'It's short for Euphemia. She was named after Morag's own mother. In fact, the name has passed down in our family from one generation to the next. My mother's called Effie too but she made a change with me. She thought Effie

27

would sound a bit too old-fashioned. Dad was the one who suggested Eileen. Are you descended from Effie too? She had fourteen children.'

'No, not Effie. Donald's our man. He was my grandfather and he came right at the very end of Morag's big family. "Wee Donald", they called him. Some of his older sisters and brothers were grown up and married by the time he was born. Wee Donald himself married very young and only had one child. That was my father. We're the MacRaes, by the way. Bob and Gill MacRae from Hobart in Tassy.'

'We're the Gallaghers,' said Eileen in return. 'We live up in the Mallee. These are my brothers, Kevin and Jack. Mum always says our ancestor Morag was the best of the bunch! I'm so glad you come from the very same family, Mr MacRae.'

'Aw, look, there's no need for *Mr* MacRae. Just call me Bob. And your mother's absolutely right about Morag being the best of the bunch. Morag was the one who saw the coffin in the bush, you know.'

'Saw what?' shrieked Jack.

'The coffin. I thought your mother would've told you that story. My grandfather was always telling me. He said that when Morag was a girl of about thirteen she was sitting by the edge of a creek when she saw four tall Highlanders carrying a coffin through the bush. She called out to them but they didn't answer. It was a sign, you know. A sign that a death was coming. And sure enough, a few weeks later, some poor old lady died. Friend of the family, she was.'

Kevin started to laugh but Eileen stopped him with a glance.

'Did she *really* see the coffin?' she asked.

'She was sure she did but no one else saw it. Morag

always told her children that was the day when she knew she had the second sight.'

'What's the second sight?' asked Eileen, a strange prickling of her skin at the back of her neck. The bare-footed girl on the school bus flashed across her memory.

'It's all moonshine!' said Gill MacRae crossly.

'No, no, it's not moonshine, Gill,' said Bob. 'Some people from the Highlands and islands of Scotland really do have it. They *see* things that no one else can see. They *know* things no one else can know. The second sight's a gift passed down in a family, often through the women. Sometimes it skips a generation but it never gets completely lost. But let's forget about all that now. You three kids aren't camping here on your own, are you?'

Eileen shook her head. 'Mum and Dad are with us,' she said. 'Those are our three little green tents over there. Do come and meet Mum, Bob. She'll be thrilled to find another of Morag's descendants.'

The two gnomes walked across the camping ground between Eileen and Kev. Jack ran on ahead.

'Mum!' he shouted. 'We've found your rellies!'

It was a happy meeting. There was so much to say. Mum sat next to Bob MacRae and Dad took their photo. They certainly did look alike. You could see they were cousins of some sort. Mum might almost have been Bob's daughter.

'It's the eyes,' Dad said, gazing at the two of them.

'No, I think it's the chin,' said Gill with a smile. 'A stubborn kind of chin.'

'But your girl there,' said Bob. 'Your Eileen. *She's* the one with the family face. Let's bring her into the photo too.'

'So like our poor Anna,' Gill said sadly, her mood suddenly changing. 'She died, you know. Just a year ago, it was.'

'Oh, Gill!' Mum cried. 'What a terrible thing to happen! I'm so sorry.' She put her arms round Gill and hugged her as if she'd known her all her life.

Eileen felt thankful that Mum had known what to say and what to do. She smiled across at Gill in relief.

'You don't have the family Bible, do you?' Dad asked Bob MacRae. 'We've got that old foot-plough up on the roof of the car there. We're sure someone must have the Bible.'

Bob shook his head. 'Nothing like that,' he said. 'All we've got is a sort of a necklace. Made of emu feathers and stitched to a band of possum skin. Aboriginal work, they told us at the museum in Hobart. It's getting a bit frail now so we have to handle it carefully. Belonged to Morag MacDonald in the early days, so my father always said.'

'Goodness knows how she came to have it,' said Gill. 'I only hope she didn't steal it.'

'Did you bring the necklace with you?' Eileen asked excitedly. 'Will you let us see it?'

Gill looked at Bob and he nodded.

'Of course,' she said. 'It's in our caravan. Come across and have a look.'

Eileen held the ancient necklace in her fingers. She stroked the soft feathers, brown at the stem where they were stitched to the band and paler at the tip.

'It's so beautiful,' she breathed. 'Could I put it on? Just for a minute?'

Gill hesitated but then she smiled. 'All right. I always used to let Anna put it on. Here, I'll tie it for you at the back. There we are. It looks fine.'

The emu feathers lay gently around Eileen's neck. A curious shiver ran through her whole body. The distant past seemed much closer, somehow. Suddenly that bare-footed girl on the bus came darting back into her mind again. The bare-footed girl and the scent of aniseed. Or something like aniseed. If there ever really *was* a girl on the bus. Eileen pulled her drifting thoughts back to the MacRaes and to the emu feathers.

'I do wish this lovely thing had come down in *our* family,' she said wistfully, unfastening the necklace. 'It's so much better than that ugly old foot-plough.'

'Everyone has something,' said Gill, passing the heirloom to each of the others in turn and then putting it safely away in its cardboard box. 'Something to keep the memories alive. That's all that matters. We're not going to put this necklace out for everyone else at the gathering to gawp at but we're very glad for you to see it. Bob's got just one other scrap of a memory from the past but it's not much use. He says his father used to tell him an old family story about two brothers called Donald. Dark Donald and Fair Donald. They were fishermen and they lived in a little black house on the edge of a great sea loch. That's all he can remember. It's not much to go on, is it?'

'I've never heard that one,' said Eileen, her eyes lighting up. 'But Mum's got a tiny bit of an old Skye story about a terrible storm. She only knows a couple of lines of it. "The wind raged and the thunder roared. The lightning flashed and the rain beat down!" It's become a family saying but I do wish she knew the rest.'

'How come you three kids aren't at school?' Bob asked them as Gill made a pot of tea. 'It's not holidays, is it?'

'No,' Eileen said. 'The schools gave us a whole week off. Ten days if we need it. They said this trip would do us good.'

'So it will,' said Gill. 'You're bound to learn a lot.'

'More than you bargained for, probably,' Dad chuckled.

'When families get together they find out some odd things. Old secrets get uncovered.'

Eileen thought about Rex Woodburn's castle. Rex might be in for a nasty shock if anyone told him the truth about the little black house.

'We've all got to give talks at school when we get back,' said Kev proudly. 'About this family gathering.' Kev thought he was rather good at giving talks. He was actually looking forward to it and he'd already started making notes.

'Mine's going to be called "Meeting a Thousand Cousins",' Eileen said with a smile.

'Well, you've made a good start,' said Bob as Gill poured the tea into a row of mugs. 'You've met us. Only nine hundred and ninety-eight more to go!'

Everyone laughed.

'Do you know anyone else who's coming to the gathering, Bob?' Mum asked him.

There was an awkward pause.

'No,' he said at last. 'I'm an only child myself and so was my father. I've never known anyone else from Morag's family. To tell you the truth, Effie, there was some kind of trouble among the MacRaes. Haven't you ever heard about it? A long time ago it was. Just at the beginning of the First World War in nineteen fourteen, soon after Morag died. I don't know what started it but the family split from top to bottom. Your old Effie and the other sisters weren't involved in the quarrel, I'm glad to say, but my wee Donald was cut off from all his older brothers. He'd never say a good word about any of them, so my dad always told me.'

Mum was stunned.

'I'm very sorry, Bob,' she said. 'I had no idea. My mother certainly never mentioned any quarrel. But perhaps you'll meet some of our other relations on Saturday and we'll be able to sort it all out, whatever it was.'

'I don't think so,' said Bob gloomily. 'These old family feuds are hard to heal. The man I really want to meet is Rex Woodburn. The chap who's organized this whole thing. He's got an amazing flair for getting things moving, hasn't he? He's a *real* MacDonald, I reckon, even if his name's Woodburn.'

After the hot tea came a brilliant hour in the sea off Smith's Beach. The MacRaes joined the Gallaghers in the water. Eileen was surprised to see that the 'retired gnomes', as she'd called them at first, were expert surfers in the old-fashioned way, without any bother of boards. They simply put their heads down, stretched out their arms in front and leapt into each wave. She wished she moved as easily in the rough sea as they did.

'This is a bit better than the pool at home!' Kev yelled to the others, catching a great green breaker.

Much more exciting, Eileen thought to herself as the water tumbled her violently to the shore, but not quite so safe.

That evening, as Mum and Bob sat by the barbecue talking over their family recollections, Eileen lay on her back looking up at the stars. Suddenly her eye caught a glimpse of a shadowy figure moving about the camping ground. She sat up. A girl was running silently between the tents, darting from one cluster of people to the next, pausing only for a second or two and then running on. An old-fashioned sort of girl in a plain dark dress with long sleeves and a white scarf knotted around her neck.

'Stop!' Eileen called out loud.

The girl stopped and stared at her.

'Who *are* you?' Eileen called.

33

There was no answer. The girl bounded away like a startled rabbit.

'Eileen!' Mum said sharply, looking over her shoulder. 'Who on earth are you shouting at?'

'No one,' Eileen said. She lay down again, her heart pounding. She gazed up at the stars with puzzled tears in her eyes. A faint scent of aniseed hung in the air.

4

Jo Woodburn

By Friday morning, Malcolm had recovered from the long flight. The floor no longer heaved under his feet. His head had stopped spinning. He could sleep peacefully without waking up suddenly in the middle of the night.

'Lucky we're both having a few days off work, Jan,' Uncle Don said at breakfast. 'I wouldn't want to miss this meeting with Rex Woodburn.'

'He might be awful, Dad,' said Chloë.

'No, he sounds a cheerful sort of man,' said her father. 'He's certainly a good organizer, anyway. Look how he put those notices in the newspapers all over Australia asking for any descendants of Donald and Effie MacDonald to get in touch with him. And look how he wrote back to everyone and booked Queen's Park for Saturday and arranged the church service and the trip up to Brolga Marsh and the old family mansion and everything else. It's amazing what he's done.'

'That place Brolga Marsh came into one of Morag's letters,' said Malcolm, suddenly remembering. 'She called it a sheep-run. Is "brolga" another word for sheep?'

Everyone laughed. Malcolm felt foolish. He wished he'd asked his father that question.

'It's a bird,' Chloë explained. 'A long-legged bird that

lives by lakes and marshes. Brolgas dance, you know! There must have been hundreds of them there on the marsh in the early days.'

'A sheep-run was a huge farm for thousands of sheep,' Uncle Don said to Malcolm. 'We might call it a sheep-station these days or just a property. In Scotland you'd call it an estate, I think. Brolga Marsh lies west of Ballarat, not far from Linton, and it's certainly huge. I can see why Morag thought it was as big as the Isle of Skye but she did exaggerate quite a bit. Your dad's probably told you how our ancestors went to work there as shepherds and domestic servants when they first arrived in the colony. Rex Woodburn's been in touch with the present owner of Brolga Marsh and the man's perfectly happy for us all to come and have a look at the place. Very decent of him.'

'But what I can't understand is why Rex wants to see us *today*,' Malcolm said. 'Couldn't he wait till tomorrow at the big gathering?'

Uncle Don rubbed his hands together in delight. 'He says he wants to meet just one family in advance. Someone who might give him a bit of help on the day.'

'Why pick on us?' asked Chloë.

'He chose the person who wrote the best letter!' crowed Uncle Don, beaming around at them all complacently. 'Though I say it myself, I do write a good letter!'

'Dad! You're impossible!' said Chloë, her green eyes laughing.

'You're just like your big brother,' Malcolm said. 'My dad's always saying he's a brilliant teacher.'

'But so he is, Malcolm, and before that he was a brilliant barrister. We're a remarkable family, you know. It's all those MacDonald genes.'

Uncle Don didn't seem to be joking. He meant what he said. Malcolm wasn't sure whether to be amused or embarrassed. It certainly wasn't the Scottish way to praise yourself and your own family in that extraordinary fashion. Dad was bad enough at boasting but Uncle Don was even worse.

As they drove through the wide, sunny streets of Geelong to the Eastern Beach, Malcolm thought it looked a comfortable sort of town. He liked the houses built of white weatherboard or warm red brick. He liked the shady verandas, the splendid post office and the blue sky. He only wished Fiona could see it all.

'Rex Woodburn reckons our ancestors landed some-where near here,' Uncle Don said as he parked the car under trees near the edge of Corio Bay. 'He wants to meet us at the very spot where they first stepped on to Australian soil. These gardens by the Eastern Beach are the closest we'll get to it. Rex'll have a couple of blue flags in his hand so we're sure to find him easily enough.'

'Blue flags?' Malcolm murmured to Chloë. She raised one reddish eyebrow.

'They're just like children, these men,' she said quietly. Malcolm nodded and smiled back at her. He quite liked having a cousin.

'There he is!' cried Uncle Don excitedly, leaping out of the car and almost running towards an enormous man who stood in the centre of the green lawn, clutching a tall blue flag in each hand. Sprawled on the grass beside him lay a heavy, ungainly boy who looked as if he didn't want to be there at all. His eyes were turned away towards the sea. A skinny, pleasant-faced girl clung to the big man's elbow with her left hand. Her right arm was swathed in a gaudy tartan sling. All three of them had hair so fair it was almost white.

Malcolm stared in amazement at Rex Woodburn. Never in his life had he seen anyone so huge. Rex was a mountain of a man, massive and powerful. He had rolled up his sleeves to make the most of the sunshine. His long, bare arms were decorated with an intricate network of tattoos from wrist to shoulder. Perhaps, Malcolm thought to himself, he had once been a wrestler or a heavyweight boxer. The red horizontal stripes on his shirt only emphasized his girth. Uncle Don shook him warmly by the hand and introduced Aunty Jan and then Chloë and Malcolm.

'Meet me twins,' Rex Woodburn boomed proudly. 'Andy and Jo. They don't look much alike, but twins they certainly are. Turned fourteen just last week. The three of us came down to Geelong a couple of days early to make sure everything runs nice and smooth for the big gathering.'

Now Rex turned to Malcolm. 'So this is the boy from Scotland,' he said, gently taking the girl's hand away from his elbow and laying one heavy arm across Malcolm's shoulder. 'What a great day for all the MacDonalds! You'll bring a touch of the Old Country to our celebrations. Here you are, lad. Grab hold of this flag for Allan's family.'

Malcolm gripped the blue flag, pressing the pole's sharpened end into the grass at his feet. He felt rather foolish standing there with a flag. Chloë laughed softly. Was she laughing at him, he wondered, or at those curious twins, one stout and one thin, with their peculiar, spiky, white hair? His face felt hot. He looked up at the yellow letters painted on the flag.

ALLAN MACDONALD MARRIED KIRSTY
(GORDON) NICOLSON,
GEELONG, 1860. SIX LIVING CHILDREN.

'They c-can't be still living!' Malcolm protested, his stammer coming back unexpectedly. 'Allan's s-six children must have all d-died long ago.'

Rex gave a deep thunderous laugh. 'No, no! I didn't mean they were still alive, Mal. I just meant they didn't die when they were children. Those six kids of Allan's grew up, safe and sound. There might have been others who died young. Most families had a few infant deaths in the early days. Now I'll just tell you what I'd like you and your Uncle Don to do tonight. I want you to make six smaller flags, one for each of Allan's children. Then, at the gathering tomorrow, you can rally his descendants into separate family groups. You do *know* the names of Allan's six children, don't you, Don?'

'Oh yes, we know all that,' Uncle Don said proudly. 'My father had a passion for drawing up his family tree, so we know every name and who married whom. He always told us that Allan and Kirsty had met each other on Skye even before they went on board that ship, the *Georgiana*. Kirsty Gordon lived in a quarry or so the story goes, but I'm not sure if I believe that bit. Her mother was a widow with three children and she married a man called Nicolson from the ship. He had some kids of his own, I think. Families were terribly complicated in those days.'

'They're quite complicated these days,' Aunty Jan said quietly.

Malcolm's eyes slid from Allan's flag to the one Rex was still holding.

FLORA MACDONALD MARRIED JOHN
WOODBURN, 1866.
EIGHT LIVING CHILDREN.

'Did they meet on the ship, sir?' he asked the big man, not sure how he should address him. 'Your Flora and John Woodburn?'

'Sir!' Rex roared in amazement, his whole vast frame shaking with laughter. 'No need to call me "sir", lad. We don't have no sirs here. I'm just plain Rex. Call me Uncle Rex if it makes you feel better, but never "sir"!'

'S-sorry,' said Malcolm. He wished he'd never used the stupid word. He certainly wasn't going to call this man 'Uncle'. Plain 'Rex' would have to do.

'No, they didn't meet on the ship,' Rex added more calmly. 'John Woodburn wasn't on the *Georgiana*. He was English. Came from Kent. They met in Ballarat, though I don't know what on earth our Flora was doing there. Terribly rough place, it was in those days. Anyway, she didn't stay long. The day after she married John Woodburn they set off for Echuca in a bullock-cart.'

'Where's Echuca?' Malcolm asked. He was rather hazy about Australian geography.

'Up on the Murray River, lad. You should know that. Your dad hasn't taught you proper. John Woodburn found good work up there, first with the big draught horses and then with the paddle-steamers on the river. He lived in Echuca with Flora for fifty years till the day he died. Flora ran a little school in the house as well as bringing up her eight children. A wonderful teacher, our Flora was. Everyone says so.'

'Have you got any heirlooms, Rex?' Chloë asked him. 'Anything passed on to you from those early days.'

'Only me little milk-jug, that's all. A funny, cracked, white milk-jug from the Isle of Skye. Effie MacDonald gave it to our Flora on her wedding day. But I've got me photos of the castle, of course. Our family castle on Skye or the remains of it. I was over there last year on me trip

40

and I found the place near Talisker. I only had to ask the locals and they soon showed me the pile of stones where our castle used to stand.'

'But our ancestors didn't live in a castle!' Malcolm blurted out before he could stop himself. 'They lived in a smoky black house like all the other crofters. A kind of a hut. I've brought an old photo to show you.'

Rex's jovial air faded at once. 'You must be wrong about that, Mal. Our Flora was born in a castle all right. Her children always said so and I've seen the place with me own eyes. I've got the photos to prove it.'

Malcolm opened his mouth to protest again but Aunty Jan squeezed his arm hard to stop him.

'Now!' said Rex, suddenly pleasant once more. 'I've hired a boat down at the marina for an hour or two. I want to take you all out into the bay till we're opposite Point Henry. That's where the *Georgiana* dropped anchor in eighteen fifty-two after three months at sea. And that's where the whole crew rose up against the captain because they wanted to go to the gold-diggings at Ballarat. You've heard about the terrible mutiny, I suppose.'

Everyone nodded. That frightening story had been passed down in every branch of the family.

'The cook was shot dead,' said Malcolm. 'Dad told me. And our Allan was very brave.'

Everyone nodded again.

'When we've been out as far as Point Henry, we'll turn round and come back to the shore,' Rex went on, 'so we'll be following the journey our family took when they landed. A kind of a pilgrimage.'

Malcolm's heart lifted a bit. He liked this idea of going out on the water in a boat. He was even more relieved when Rex offered to stow the two flags in his car. The bay was choppy. The outboard motor roared and the little boat bounced over the shallow waves. Malcolm was sitting next to Jo.

'Look!' he cried out excitedly, pointing ahead. 'That must be Point Henry!'

She turned her face towards him. 'Yes,' she said with a friendly smile. 'Dad brought Andy and me out here yesterday for a trial run. That's when I fell over in the boat and hurt my arm.'

'Is it serious?' Malcolm asked her with a frown of concern.

'No, not really. Dad said it wasn't worth bothering a doctor. The wrist's a bit swollen and painful, that's all, so Dad fixed up this sling for me. He had to use my tartan scarf. He couldn't find anything else.'

She giggled a bit and put her good hand over her pale mouth. Malcolm couldn't help laughing quietly himself. He'd never seen a tartan sling before. It looked ridiculous but he quite liked this girl. She was different.

'Your dad seems to love the sea,' he said, watching the skilful way Rex handled the boat and the contented smile on his broad face.

'He *does* love the sea! He used to work on the big cargo ships when he was young and he's never quite got used to living on solid land again. He wants Andy to go to sea.'

'Andy!' Malcolm said in surprise, keeping his voice down. 'I can't imagine Andy as a sailor.'

Jo grinned at him. 'You're right! Andy hates the sea. But since Mum died four years ago, Dad's never got on too well with Andy. He can't grasp the simple fact that the boy doesn't want to go to sea at all. What Andy really wants is to help our cousins run their fruit stall at Victoria Market. He loves that market. It's his second home.'

Malcolm thought of his own father who couldn't grasp the simple fact that he wanted to be a vet, not a lawyer.

Perhaps all the fathers in this family were the same!

Now Rex was shouting to them cheerfully over the noise of the engine. 'This bay was full of empty ships when our people first sailed in. All the crews had run off to the gold-diggings. Now this must be about the spot where the *Georgiana* was anchored. Somewhere near here.'

Malcolm gazed down respectfully at the green water but he felt no rush of excitement. One patch of sea looked much like another to him.

Rex turned the boat in a wide circle and directed it back more slowly towards the shore. The lovely city lay spread out before them, shining in the sunlight.

'Geelong didn't look nothing like that in eighteen fifty-two,' he bellowed. 'It was only a scruffy little town. I bet our ancestors were disappointed when they landed. After the castle on Skye, it must've been a terrible comedown to arrive at a godforsaken place like this.'

Aunty Jan gave Malcolm a firm look across the boat. To his surprise, Jo suddenly moved a bit closer and leant lightly against him for a minute or two.

'Dad's obsessed with his stupid castle,' she whispered. 'Just take no notice. He goes wild if we contradict him. I'll tell you more about it later.'

Malcolm nodded. This girl was so much nicer than her disagreeable brother who sat hunched by the rail, frowning at the sea and never saying a word. She was quite tough too. He admired the way she made no fuss at all about her sore wrist.

Rex turned the moment of landing into a kind of ceremony. He heaved himself on to the jetty and secured the boat. Then he held out a broad hand to help each of the others ashore.

'Welcome to the new country,' he declaimed, as if he were greeting the bewildered immigrants from Skye in

1852. 'Welcome to Australia! The land of opportunity! Work hard and you'll make a fortune!'

Uncle Don laughed. 'I'm afraid none of Allan's lot made a fortune, or none that I know of,' he said. 'My brother was doing pretty well as a barrister in Melbourne but then he threw it all up and moved to Scotland.'

Malcolm saw Andy giving Jo a slight flick of a wink but Jo made no response. Now Rex was talking again, his big chest swelling even bigger with pride.

'Well, *I* haven't done too badly for meself,' he said. 'But Morag's family was the one with the real money. Four of her sons really did make a fortune between them and they kept the dear old lady in comfort on her farm to the end of her days. But that money led to some sort of trouble, so my grandad told me. Some terrible quarrel. I don't know what it was about. We've got lots of Morag's people coming to the gathering tomorrow so I'm hoping to find out more about it when I meet them. Most of them are staying in the very best hotels in Geelong so there must still be money in Morag's family somewhere!'

'Morag's family!' cried Uncle Don in excitement. 'Just wait till those people see the letters Malcolm's brought out from Scotland.'

'Letters from Morag?' Rex's eyes flashed with new interest. 'About their family quarrel?'

'No, nothing about any quarrel but the letters come from Morag all right. She wrote them back in eighteen fifty-two when she was just a girl on the ship and then on that sheep-run near Linton. Fascinating letters!'

'What about the fourth letter, Dad?' Chloë asked him. 'That's much more fascinating.'

Her father seemed suddenly irritated. 'No, no! I won't be showing *that* one to Morag's people,' he said. 'It's only meant for Allan's people. *Our* people. That letter's private

44

family business and no concern of Morag's lot at all. Morag may have been very fond of her older brother but she always thought she knew what was best for everyone.'

'Perhaps she did know best,' said Malcolm. 'After all, she begged him not to go off on that expedition where he dis –'

'That's quite enough,' said Uncle Don harshly, breaking in before Malcolm could finish his sentence.

'I wish we had some letters from our Flora,' Rex said with a sigh of envy. 'Flora was clever enough to write letters, of course, but I suppose she was just too busy with the children and the school. I do know there used to be a wonderful old story in our family that came from Flora all those years ago. Something about a poor little black cat, drenched with the rain. My father could only re-member one line of it. "Come in, come in, little cat. You must sit by our fire." That's all I know. The rest's been lost.'

'Someone at the gathering might know more of it,' said Chloë.

Rex nodded. He looked pleased.

'Don,' he said, 'your Morag was always a bit special in that family, wasn't she? Me old grandfather used to say she had the second sight.'

'What's that?' Andy asked, speaking for the first time. Malcolm heard a sneer in his voice.

'It's a kind of a gift, I think,' said Rex, uncertainly. 'It means you can look into the future and see trouble coming. Me grandfather told me that when Morag was still only a girl, she saw four tall men carrying a long box through the bush. Or she thought she saw them anyway. It was a sign that someone was going to die.'

Now Andy laughed out loud.

'Horrible!' Aunty Jan exclaimed with a shudder.

45

'It's not always horrible,' said Malcolm, smiling reassuringly at his aunt. 'People with the second sight sometimes see friendly ghosts from the past.'

'Ghosts!' Andy guffawed, staring at Malcolm in amazement.

Chloë broke in quickly. 'Malkie, maybe you'll catch that second sight from someone in Scotland.'

Malcolm laughed. 'You don't exactly catch it,' he said. 'Some people are just born with it.'

'I wish I could have it!' said Chloë.

'Be thankful you haven't!' said Aunty Jan. 'Who wants to see back into the past or look forward into the future? It must be very unsettling to have a gift like that.'

'I don't believe a word of it!' Andy said rudely. 'Dad, I've had enough of all this family stuff. I want to go off on my own. Get some food. Buy some tapes. Ring some friends.'

Rex seemed disappointed but he soon recovered.

'All right, son,' he said. 'Do whatever you like. Just be sure to be back at our motel by six tonight. Got enough cash on you?'

Andy nodded and lumbered off towards the town. Rex turned to Aunty Jan.

'I don't quite know what to do about that boy of mine,' he said in a puzzled voice. 'He goes his own way, whatever I say. I've given him everything he wants but he still takes no notice of me.'

Aunty Jan looked as if she knew exactly what *she* would do about Andy but she held her tongue.

'Now, Don,' Rex went on, cheerful again. 'I was wondering if Chloë and Malcolm would keep an eye on Jo for me for the rest of the day. She's not so well with that bad wrist of hers. I want to take you and Jan out for a really good lunch so we can plan the final details for

46

tomorrow. These young folks would only be bored with our family talk so I suggest we just let them do their own thing.'

'Great idea!' said Uncle Don and Aunty Jan in the same breath, thinking of the lunch.

Chloë was delighted. She grinned at Malcolm and Jo. 'I could show you both round the town and we'll stop to have something to eat whenever we're hungry.'

'Let me hold your arm, Mal,' said Jo, grasping him firmly with her left hand. 'You're a quiet boy but I like you.'

The three of them set off up the steep road to the town centre. Malcolm quite liked the touch of Jo's hand on his arm. She seemed to trust him. Chloë led the way to the Wool Museum, the art gallery and a music shop reverberating with Mozart. They stopped often to have something to eat. Jo seemed to be enjoying every minute of it. She never stopped smiling.

'Now,' she said at the third café where they sat down for yet another cup of coffee, another slice of cake. 'Let's talk about Dad's stupid castle.'

'What about it?' asked Chloë, pushing both hands upward through her springy red hair till it stuck out around her face like a halo.

'Poor old Dad! He invented the whole idea a few years ago. It was just before Mum died. He'd heard from his grandfather or someone about those terrible little huts on Skye that you were talking about, Mal. Mum told me he hated to think of his precious ancestors living in a place like that.'

'With the cow,' put in Malcolm.

'A cow!' Jo gasped, looking straight into Malcolm's eyes. 'A cow inside the hut! Don't tell him about the cow, whatever you do! He couldn't bear it.'

'Why's he so fussy?' asked Chloë. 'My dad doesn't mind about the hut or the cow. He says we've done very well for ourselves over the years. He says we've come a long way from that hut.'

'I think I know why my dad's so fussy,' said Jo. 'You see, he had a terrible struggle when he was a kid. He pretty well lived in a hut himself, up there in Echuca where his ancestors had settled. It was a rough sort of shack anyway. Then, when he'd worked on the cargo ships for a few years, he left the sea and started up a little business of his own. That's when his whole life changed. Everything he touched seemed to turn to gold, he always says. Once he'd begun to do so well and bought a new house for us and everything, he didn't like to think of his poor old family coming from a hut, so he made up the castle. Not long after Mum died he went on his big trip to Skye. The people over there were only too glad to tell him that some heap of stones he'd found was once a castle. I bet they were laughing their heads off! They must get lots of tourists searching for castles. And Dad's been talking about that castle ever since. He really believes in it.'

'So you think I'd better keep quiet about the black house?' said Malcolm, disappointed. 'Dad gave me a photo to show everyone.'

Jo laughed. 'Most of the family'll love to see it, Mal,' she said. 'Show it to all the others but not to my dad. Just keep quiet when he starts talking about his castle. I want a peaceful weekend. Now, is there anywhere we can go bowling?'

'Bowling!' exclaimed Malcolm, staring at her tartan sling. 'But you've hurt your right arm. Are you left-handed?'

'No,' Jo said, 'but I can have a go with my left hand, can't I? I'm beginning to get a bit tired of all these educational sights. No more museums or art galleries, thanks! No more Mozart!'

'Sorry,' said Chloë with a shrug. 'There's a ten-pin bowling alley just along the road. If you're sure that's what you want.'

'Absolutely sure,' Jo said, pushing away her cup and standing up.

'Come on then, Malkie,' said Chloë. 'We'll see who's best. The Aussies or the Jocks!'

Malcolm suddenly flamed into anger.

'Don't call me Jock!' he barked at her. 'I hate it! That's what the English call us! Don't you know it's racist? It's as bad as calling black people niggers!'

'Sorry!' gasped Chloë, startled at his fury. 'Honestly, I didn't know.'

Jo took his arm again. His anger melted away.

Malcolm had never been bowling in his life before. He didn't do too badly for a first attempt. Chloë was a bit more practised but it was Jo who handled the balls with such casual ease and sent them spinning down the alley with uncanny accuracy.

'However do you do it?' Malcolm asked her in amazement as the pins tumbled at the far end. 'And with your left hand too.'

'Dad taught me when I was just a little kid. He made me bowl sometimes with one hand and sometimes with the other. He says I can do anything if I try.'

'He's right,' said Malcolm, looking at Jo in admiration. 'I reckon you could do anything you wanted.'

Jo smiled happily. Malcolm couldn't help noticing her teeth. So even and straight and white and well-looked-after. Everyone in this country seemed to have such perfect teeth. Was it because of the good dentists, he wondered, or was it the fruit they were always eating? He'd been astonished to see Uncle Don and Aunty Jan munching their way through a couple of apples at the end of every meal. It was almost a ritual.

At that moment Malcolm thought he caught a glimpse of Andy, standing at the doorway to the bowling rink and staring at Jo, but in a moment he had gone, if he was ever there at all. In any case, Jo suddenly seemed to have had enough of the bowling.

'What could we do next?' she asked.

'Let's go and look at the family lion,' Chloë suggested. 'It's outside the Town Hall.'

Malcolm looked alarmed.

'Not a real one, Malkie,' laughed Chloë. 'It's made of stone.'

They trudged along to the Town Hall together, Jo's hand on Malcolm's arm again and Chloë leading the way. Malcolm was weary now but he didn't really want this afternoon to end. There were two stone lions at the Town Hall, one on each side of a flight of steps. Under the lion on the left was a plaque in memory of a couple of MacDonalds who were somehow part of their family history. They'd died years ago. Chloë read the words out aloud.

'Let me feel it,' Jo insisted, reaching up to the lion, her pale blue eyes alert and shining.

She put her good hand on the lion's head. Carefully she felt the eyes, the mane, the mouth, the teeth. She ran her fingers along his back and right to his tail. Then the paws. Then back to his mouth again. She looked very hard at the mouth.

'Is he smiling at us, Mal? What do you think?'

'Not exactly smiling,' said Malcolm, pleased that she'd asked him. 'I think he looks quite fierce. As if he's just resting before he springs for the kill!'

Jo laughed. 'That sounds like our family all right!' she said. 'Mal, could you get me a taxi? It's time I was going back to the motel. Dad never likes me to be late.'

Malcolm and Chloë put Jo into her taxi and then caught a bus home.

'She's not short of money, is she?' Chloë said wistfully as their bus sped out to the edge of the town, pulling up suddenly at every stop and then leaping forward again like an impatient horse. 'I think you and I have been born into the wrong bit of the family somehow, Malkie.'

'I quite liked her,' said Malcolm cautiously.

'I could see that!' Chloë said, smiling at him in amusement. 'You'd better not tell Fiona.'

'Of course I'll tell Fiona!' Malcolm was indignant. 'This Jo's only a cousin and a very distant cousin at that. I'm just sorry for her, that's all. Her mother's dead. And she's got that awful brother. And she's hurt her arm.'

'I wonder,' murmured Chloë, half closing her eyes.

5

Fennel

'Anyone up yet?' a voice called loudly by the Gallaghers' tents, early on that same Friday morning.

Eileen stuck her head out through the door of her tent. Gill MacRae was standing there, stocky and small, in black gumboots, black trousers and white shirt. Her grey hair was wrapped up in a bright green scarf.

'I'm awake,' Eileen said, smiling up at Gill. 'I'm just reading in bed.'

'Bob and I are going on a kind of pilgrimage today. Back to the place near Mount Macedon where those old ancestors of yours and Bob's used to live. You know, Morag MacDonald and Rory MacRae. We wondered if you and the two boys would like to come with us.'

'I'd love to come,' Eileen said at once. 'Hang on a minute and I'll ask Kev and Jack.'

She ran over the grass in bare feet to the boys' tent. Kev and Jack were not the slightest bit interested in going on a pilgrimage. They muttered crossly at Eileen and rolled over to sleep again.

'Sorry, only me,' she told Gill. 'When are you leaving?'

'In about half an hour.'

'I'll be ready. I'll just ask Mum if it's all right. She's sure to agree.'

Bob MacRae's car had certainly seen better days. The paintwork was scratched and the springs had gone slack but the back seat was comfortable enough. A checked brown rug covered the gaps in the leather upholstery. Eileen settled into her corner as Bob drove out of the camping ground and took the road for Geelong and then the freeway towards Melbourne. The day was sunny but not yet too hot.

Bob and Gill were a strangely silent couple, Eileen thought. They didn't talk to each other all the time the way Mum and Dad did but it was a fairly comfortable sort of silence. She decided not to break it with her usual burble.

'How old are you, Eileen?' Gill asked suddenly as Bob left the freeway near Werribee and swung north towards Woodend.

'Thirteen,' said Eileen.

'Just the age our Anna would have been,' Bob said. 'When's your birthday?'

'April.'

'So was Anna's,' said Gill. 'We didn't see her very often, you know. Our son lives right over in Western Australia so we kept in touch with Anna by telephone calls and letters. But he always used to bring her across to us for one week every September. That was always a wonderful week for us. The best week of the whole year.'

Eileen felt distinctly awkward with all this talk about Anna. She didn't want Bob and Gill to treat her as some kind of double of their granddaughter. She was just herself. Eileen Gallagher. Silence fell again in the car and this time it was not quite so comfortable.

Halfway between Hanging Rock and Mount Macedon, Bob found the place he was looking for. It lay off a narrow dirt track that climbed up steeply from the road. In the bottom corner of a wooded paddock stood a solitary brick chimney, all that was left of an early homestead. What had once been a garden was now overgrown with tall feathery leaves, thick as a green forest. Nothing else. No crumbling walls. No footpaths. Not even a doorstep.

'Come and see,' said Bob.

Eileen stepped right in among the weeds, looking up at the soft leaves over her head. They had an odd smell, those weeds. A bit like aniseed.

'Fennel,' said Gill, sniffing at the strong smell. 'I'm sure Morag herself must have been the one who planted it years ago but now it's run completely wild. Just look! It's taken over the house as well as the garden.'

'When exactly did Morag come here, Bob?' Eileen asked.

'Straight after she married Rory in eighteen sixty. They simply squatted on this piece of land to start with and lived in a tent. Later they were able to buy the land for themselves and they stayed here for the rest of their lives. It was always a very small farm and they never made much money out of it. Barely enough to live on. After their tent had been blown to bits in a storm they put up a little log hut. That was the usual thing in those days. First the tent and then the hut. Finally Rory built a bigger house with a veranda on four sides and enough room to sleep all the children. It must've been a lovely homestead but there's nothing left of it now except this poor old chimney and the forest of fennel.'

'I quite *like* the smell,' Eileen said, surprised at herself, breaking off a leafy stem of fennel and rubbing it between her fingers. 'Peculiar but nice.'

'I can't think why Morag ever planted the wretched stuff,' Gill said crossly. 'What could anyone do with fennel?'

'Eat it?' suggested Eileen.

Gill wrinkled her nose in disgust. 'Never!' she said. 'It's some *foreign* kind of weed. Not Australian. Not even Scottish.'

'Does someone in our family still own this land?' Eileen asked, pushing the sprig of fennel into her pocket and looking up towards the herd of sleek cattle grazing contentedly at the top end of the paddock.

'No,' said Bob, shaking his head. 'I don't know who owns it now. The farm and the house were sold off soon after Morag died. Rory had been dead for about five years by then. Wee Donald, my grandfather, looked after her here for those last five years. She always said she wanted to stay in the place where she'd lived so long and so happily with Rory.'

'Bob, how can you possibly know what Morag said?' Eileen asked, laughing out loud. 'She died before you were born! You said she died in nineteen fourteen.'

'My father told me what she said, Eileen. He was her grandson and he knew her well when he was a boy. He was only about eight years old when his own mother died so my grandfather, wee Donald, brought him straight back here to Morag. She was a widow by then. It must have been about nineteen oh-nine. My father loved his Granny Morag, you see. He went on talking about her till he was an old man himself. He knew exactly what she said. He heard her speak. He knew this house when it still *was* a house.'

'Do stop, Bob!' Gill said sharply. 'You know you only get miserable when you talk on and on about your father and your grandfather. Just forget all about them! I want to walk up to the top of this paddock to see the view over the valley. Won't you come with me? And you too, Eileen?'.

Eileen wasn't quite sure why she wanted to stay by the chimney rather than climb the slope of the big paddock with Gill and Bob. Perhaps, she thought, the strange scent of fennel was holding her there.

'Don't sit in the direct sunlight, Eileen!' Gill warned her. 'Keep in the shade of that weed. We won't be long.'

The fennel grew right to the hearth's edge. Eileen sat with her back against the chimney, with the green fronds bending between her face and the hot sun. The smell of the weed was overpowering. She closed her eyes.

'So you've come at last, girl!' said a voice.

Eileen woke at once. A woman sat close beside her. An elderly woman with silvery hair and a lined face under the brim of a brown straw hat. There was something familiar about those dark shining eyes. Eileen stared.

'You've come at last!' said the woman again.

'I-I think you must have the wrong person. Who are you waiting for?' Eileen edged away from her, along the cool hearth.

'For you, dear. I thought someone from the family would be sure to come. I just waited.'

'The family?' asked Eileen.

'The MacDonalds and the MacRaes and the Mathesons and the Nicolsons. We're all connected, you know. Skye people marry Skye people. We don't trust outsiders.'

'Are you the one who lived here?' Eileen asked her.

'Lives here.'

'The one they call Morag?'

The old woman nodded and smiled.

'I knew you'd come,' she said yet again. 'But who are you? You must be family. You've got a Skye-shaped head.'

Eileen laughed and ran her fingers over her scalp to feel its shape. 'I'm Eileen Gallagher. My mother's descended from your daughter Effie.'

'Effie was such a good girl,' said Morag, smiling as she remembered.

'If you'll just wait here for a few minutes, you could talk to Bob,' Eileen gabbled. 'Bob MacRae. His grand-father was your son Donald.'

'Poor wee Donald!' cried Morag, tears starting from her eyes. 'It's you must be setting it right, Eileen Gallagher. You're the one with the gift.'

'Setting what right?'

'My poor wee Donald was cheated! And him so kind to me in this very house. His boy was cheated too. I loved that boy! Set it right, Eileen Gallagher, set it right.'

'How can I?' gasped Eileen. 'They're all dead and gone. All your children. Ages ago!'

'Look in the cedarwood box.'

'Where is it?'

'At the turn of the stairs. In the fine big house. Some-body put it there. Safe and secure. Safe and secure.'

Eileen was confused. Which house? This broken fennel-house in the bush? There was nothing left here but the chimney.

'There's danger!' old Morag said suddenly.

'In the cedarwood box?' Eileen couldn't believe it.

'No! For the quiet boy. The Scottish boy. Allan's boy.'

'What can *I* do about it?' Eileen asked anxiously, barely keeping up with these sudden switches.

'O taste and see! That's the moment, girl. Look out for him then. Keep close to him then. O taste and see!'

'Taste what?'

'Warn the quiet boy. Keep close, keep close. He's too easily led!'

'Led where?' Eileen was utterly bewildered now.

'Emu feathers,' Morag said, her voice fainter, her eyes half closed against the heat.

57

'Oh yes!' cried Eileen, thankful to be on more familiar ground at last. 'I've seen them. They're lovely. Gill put them right round my neck.'

'Kal-Kal, the Aboriginal girl, gave me those feathers. She was my friend. And I gave her a white shell from Skye. She heard the sea in the shell.'

'Did you ever see emus running?' Eileen asked, probing at the mystery, remembering the bare-footed girl on the bus.

'Often,' murmured the old woman, so softly that Eileen could barely catch the word.

'Eileen!' shouted Gill MacRae's voice suddenly, close at hand and harsh with fear. 'Where are you? I can't see you!'

Eileen sprang to her feet in a rush of relief. 'I'm here, Gill! I haven't moved.'

Cautiously she glanced to right and left. Morag had gone.

'I'm here!' Eileen called again.

'So you are,' said Gill, thrusting the fennel stalks aside and bursting through to the chimney. 'The sun must've been in my eyes. We had a splendid view from the top. You should've come with us.'

'Sorry,' said Eileen, shivering in all the heat of the day. First that girl on the bus and now an old woman in the fennel. Had she *really* seen them? Were there two of them or only one?

'Whatever's the matter, Eileen?' cried Bob in surprise, coming up behind Gill now. 'You're trembling!'

'It's just this fennel,' Eileen said, her voice breaking oddly. 'I can't breathe!'

Bob took her arm. 'Come on,' he said, leading her out into the open. 'This is a strange place. Full of old memories. Let's drive straight to Romsey. It's a lovely little township and I know a good place where we can eat. You'll feel better when you get some food inside you.'

Eileen was utterly thankful to be back on the brown checked rug again. It was so normal, so comforting. She didn't mind the old car's rattles and jolts. The thought of food at Romsey seemed wonderful. But she couldn't quite shake off that string of mysterious words that still sang in her head.

'Set it right!' she repeated silently. 'Safe and secure! There's danger! O taste and see! Warn the quiet boy! Keep close! Emu feathers!'

She shook herself. She pushed the memory of Morag right out of her mind. Bob and Gill were silent all the way to Romsey but once they were seated around a table in the busy little café, the three of them began to talk again quite cheerfully — about the good weather, about tomorrow's gathering, about Eileen's school and the Gallaghers' farm in the Mallee. They stuffed themselves eagerly with food.

'Bob, did you say your grandfather, wee Donald, was the youngest in Morag's family?' Eileen asked him, wanting to know much more.

Bob nodded and smiled. 'The youngest of nine,' he said proudly. 'Born in eighteen eighty, he was, when Morag was just forty.'

'And he lived in a great big house with stairs and everything?'

'No, never!' Bob said, indignant and surprised. 'He worked on laying the railway tracks for about ten years after he married and he lived with his wife and the boy in a shack by the line. Then his wife died suddenly. That's when he brought his boy back to Morag in the fennel-house we saw today. I told you all that. There were no stairs at all. It was just an ordinary farmhouse with a wide veranda.'

'So poor wee Donald came running back to mother!' said Eileen with a laugh. She thought this grandfather of Bob's sounded a bit pathetic.

'She *needed* him by that time, Eileen,' said Bob. 'And his little boy needed *her*. She couldn't manage the farm on her own, once Rory had died. It was completely out of control. She refused to leave it, so our Donald looked after her and the farm as best he could. He shouldered the whole burden.'

'What about Donald's eight brothers and sisters? Didn't they help?'

'The girls were very loyal. Every one of them asked their mother to come and live with her but she wouldn't budge from the farm except for an occasional visit. The sons gave her money to live on. They had plenty to give. My father always said those four boys owned a gold mine between them, though I don't know if that could be true. Wee Donald was the one who *loved* her most. He stayed with her till she died.'

'And what happened after that?'

'I don't know,' Bob said. 'My father didn't know or perhaps he just didn't tell me. There was trouble of some kind. That's when the family split. The only thing my father passed on to me was his hatred. He said Donald had been cheated by his brothers. He said *he'd* been cheated too. He even said *I'd* been cheated!'

'Cheated!' Eileen caught at the word old Morag herself had used. If it really was Morag she'd met under the fennel. 'How was he cheated?'

'Eileen!' Bob cried in exasperation. 'I've told you! I don't know!'

'But don't you want to find out?'

'No, I don't! Now that's enough about my cursed family! We'd better head back to our camp!'

Everyone in the café looked up as the angry little man pushed his way out of the door, followed by Gill and Eileen, both embarrassed by his loud voice in such a quiet place.

No one spoke at all on the journey back to Ocean Grove. Eileen stretched herself out on the back seat of the car but she couldn't sleep. Her mind was whirling with impossible questions. Why had that old woman under the fennel chosen *her* to sort out some family quarrel from so long ago? And who was the quiet boy in danger? And how could she find the cedarwood box?

Morag's words were still nagging away inside Eileen's head. Each saying seemed to her like a little spell, a puzzling proverb, a coded message. The only one that made any sense was the last of all. 'Emu feathers.' At least she did know what the emu feathers were and where they were but not what she was supposed to do with them. As for the boy, the danger, the box, the taste – she had no idea what they meant. Her heart raced with fear and excitement as her fingers searched again for the sprig of fennel in her pocket. She pressed the feathery leaves against her nose and sniffed at the strange elusive scent. A bit like aniseed. At that moment an unexpected wave of calmness rolled over her. A high green wave like a wave of the sea. And clear as a bell, somewhere inside her head, she heard old Morag's gentle voice.

'It's you must be sorting it out, Eileen Gallagher! You're the one with the gift!'

6

The Gathering

Malcolm could hear the wild skirl of bagpipes even before he reached Queen's Park on Saturday morning. Then he saw them. A full pipe band with splendid kilts and drums and twirling drumsticks, marching in stately step up and down the whole length of the grassy oval to the strains of some triumphant war-song. Behind the band ran a mob of excited children, laughing and shouting and imitating the drum major.

It was easy to spot Rex Woodburn. He was wearing a kilt himself, MacDonald tartan of course, made in gargantuan proportions to go right round his huge waist. A new glengarry bonnet sat jauntily on his head. Malcolm thought the man looked ridiculous but Rex was clearly delighted with himself. He beamed with childlike pride and satisfaction as the long-awaited day of celebration began. Already he had placed his five blue flags at well-separated points around the edge of the oval. Already a large crowd of people was clustering by each flag, spreading rugs on the grass, unfolding deck-chairs, setting out heirlooms on the trestle tables, putting up smaller flags to represent each of their ancestor's children. Malcolm could see people kissing and embracing as they met each other with cries of astonished recognition.

Chloë was holding the six small flags for Allan's tribe, one for each of his children. Uncle Don was clutching two heavy briefcases as he bounced out of the car.

'I've photocopied the black house two hundred times!' he said to Malcolm, flourishing his bags. 'And Morag's early letters two hundred times! I'm going to give a bundle to each of the five families to distribute among themselves.'

'What about the one that tells how Allan disappeared?' Malcolm asked him.

'No, I still think it's better if we just keep that to ourselves. Here it is, Malcolm, you'd better put it in your pocket so I don't hand it over to someone by mistake. We don't want to cause any unhappiness on such a wonderful day, do we? We must just forget about Allan and remember what a great woman our Allan's *wife* was. Kirsty Nicolson. She brought up those six children single-handed after he went off on his mad adventure into the desert. She's much more important to us than old Allan ever was! But the less said about either of them the better.'

Malcolm was amused to see his uncle's sudden switch of admiration from Allan to Kirsty but he couldn't help agreeing. Kirsty must have been a tower of strength. He wondered if anyone at the gathering would know what happened to that fatherless family in Penola. Did Kirsty's six children get on well with the widower's children or were they always quarrelling? Did Kirsty ever marry the widower? That might have been a good solution.

'I'll just drop off Morag's early letters at each flag,' Uncle Don said, 'and then I'll join you in Allan's corner. Perfect weather for a family gathering, eh, Malcolm?'

Malcolm looked up. A cloudless blue sky, as always, and a warm morning sun. What an amazing country this was! So dependable. So easy to live in. How could Dad have left it?

Aunty Hen and Aunty Harriet were the first to fall on Malcolm with shouts of joy. Dad's older sisters, tall and willowy and quick-eyed. Quite gentle really. Malcolm liked them at once. He smiled as he remembered how Dad had said they were bossy. They didn't seem bossy to him.

'You look a bit like your father, Mal,' said Aunty Hen, holding him at arm's length and taking a good long look at him. 'But you're like your mother too. She was always a handsome girl. I miss her. Your dad was very foolish to go rushing off to Scotland all those years ago. He should've braved it out.'

'Braved it out?' asked Malcolm. Now at last he was getting somewhere.

'Come and meet my kids,' Aunty Harriet broke in, pushing forward a gang of five.

'Hi!' they said, staring at Malcolm with rounded eyes, as if he had come from another planet.

'Hi!' he repeated but couldn't think what to say next. The youngest of these cousins was a dark-haired little girl with her thumb in her mouth. Malcolm stooped and picked her up.

'Hi!' he said again to the tiny girl. She wriggled in his arms and squawked happily.

'Let them hear how you say "gathering", Malkie,' Chloë urged him.

'Gathering!' said Malcolm obediently before he could stop himself.

'Gathering! Gathering!' shrieked all the children in amazement, mocking his pronunciation.

'How do you say "father"?' Malcolm demanded sharply of the boy who was laughing the loudest.

'Father, of course,' said the boy cockily.

'Father. Gather. The sound's exactly the same!' said Malcolm.

The circle of children was quiet. Malcolm watched them reciting the words silently in their heads. 'Father, gather, father, gather, fathering, gathering.'

'Sorry, Malkie,' said Chloë.

'She's terribly bossy,' said one of Aunty Harriet's lot. 'She's our worst cousin. Harry's really great!'

Malcolm laughed and the tension was broken. He sat down on a tartan rug and released the child. All the others flopped close beside him and the talking began. Malcolm gazed in fascination at all these cousins of his. Each one was different – fair or dark, tall or small, thin or plump – but in every pair of eyes there was a recognizable glance, something fleeting and familiar. In every voice was a sound he seemed to know already. He really did belong to these people.

Now second cousins and third cousins and fourth cousins were flocking around Allan's flagpole. Uncle Don was in his element, shaking hands with long-lost relations, distributing copies of the black-house photograph and Morag's letters, handing over a small flag to each separate part of Allan's huge clan. Malcolm felt a sudden twinge of homesickness as the warm family voices enveloped him. Dad would have loved this day. He should have been here.

'Testing! Testing! One, two, three!' Rex Woodburn was at the microphone in the dead centre of the green oval. The pipe band was relaxing with beer under the trees.

'Welcome, one and all, to this great MacDonald family gathering!' cried Rex in triumph. 'Our ancestors sailed so far from Skye more than a hundred and forty years ago. But we're glad they came, aren't we?'

'Yes!' roared the crowd.

'And they'd be proud of us if they could see us today, wouldn't they?'

'Yes!' roared the crowd again, laughing and clapping in delight.

'And we're proud of every one of them! That wonderful couple from our castle on Skye! Donald and Effie Mac-Donald. And their four fine children. Allan, so brave and steady and strong. Morag, so full of imagination. Flora, the gifted teacher. Kenny, the inventor, the pioneer. And then there was the dear little orphan cousin, Katie, that they found in Greenock just before the ship sailed. What a lucky find she was for the whole family! Now, I want you to meet the boy who's flown all the way from Scotland to be with us today. Malcolm MacDonald – the great-great-great-grandson of Allan MacDonald! Malcolm, come right out here, lad, so everyone can see you. Here he comes! The quiet boy from Bonnie Scotland!'

The crowd began to cheer as Malcolm walked reluctantly across the wide expanse of grass to stand beside Rex Woodburn. He felt an absolute fool, dragged out in front of everyone just because he came from Scotland. These people seemed to think Scotland was some kind of religion!

'You'll all have a chance to talk with Malcolm later,' Rex said, his booming voice filling the sky. 'He'll come round to each of the flags in turn. And, of course, everyone's free to move from flag to flag. Just think how close and loving those five ancestors of ours were to each other. This is the happy day for getting to know all the branches of our wonderful family. Don't be shy! Just introduce yourself! Blood's thicker than water! Every family had better appoint someone to guard the heirlooms and mementoes. We're all honest, of course, but those old things are precious and we don't want to take any risks. Now, I'll just remind you of the programme for the rest of today and for tomorrow.'

As Rex read out his list of events – the picnic lunch

and leisurely afternoon today, the big party tonight, the church service at ten tomorrow morning up near Linton, the quick visit to Brolga Marsh and then the barbecue in the grounds of an old mansion house where someone in the family had once lived – Malcolm was no longer listening. He wanted to find Jo again before he had to start wandering about from one part of this vast family to the next. Jo never seemed to feel nervous. She always knew what to say. He'd feel safe with her. Safe and secure. His eyes searched for Flora's lot and scanned the crowd around the blue flag. There was Jo's thin face and spiky white hair! There was the tartan sling! She was holding tight to her brother's arm and looking straight across the grass towards Malcolm. He waved. Jo unhooked her left hand from Andy's elbow and waved back. Now she was beckoning to him. The minute Rex had finished his announcements, Malcolm darted across the grass towards her. When he was almost there he saw Andy bend closer to Jo, frowning, muttering, hissing right into her ear.

'Hi, Jo!' Malcolm called happily. Andy pulled away from her and moved off into the crowd. Jo smiled.

'Your dad said I have to visit every part of the family,' Malcolm said to her. 'Will you come with me?'

'Of course. But I want to start with your lot, if you don't mind. Allan's family. There's something funny going on over there. Just look!'

Malcolm stared across at the dozens of excited people milling about the six blue flags for Allan's family. There was his Aunty Jan and Uncle Don. There was Chloë, her red hair shining.

'What's so funny about them?' he asked Jo indignantly. 'They look perfectly normal to me.'

'No, no!' Jo laughed. 'Not close to the blue flags with your aunt and uncle. A good way behind that whole crowd. Just on the far side of the boundary fence. See! There's another big group. They've got a huge *yellow* flag. In fact they've got *seven* yellow flags.'

'So they have!' Malcolm said in astonishment. 'Who are they?'

'We'll soon find out!' said Jo. She took his arm and they ran full tilt towards the fence and stooped to pass under it. They pushed through the excited crowd where some people were laughing, some crying, some arguing at the tops of their voices. They came to the ring of yellow flags.

Malcolm read the words on the biggest flag out loud. 'Tom Hick married Polly Hick, eighteen seventy-nine.'

The smaller flags seemed to be for their six children: Jim Hick, born 1880; Mary Hick, born 1882; Margaret Hick, born 1883; Anne Hick, born 1889; William Hick, born 1891; John Hick, born 1894.

'How embarrassing!' Jo murmured with a grin. 'These poor people must've come to the wrong family gathering by mistake. There must be a Hick gathering somewhere else in Geelong today. They've got mixed up. How can we tell them, Mal?'

'Hullo!' said one of the dark-haired Hick boys, stepping closer and smiling at Jo with a family kind of smile that made Malcolm's heart jump. 'I love your tartan sling! Are you part of Allan's lot too?'

'But you're not MacDonalds at all, you're Hicks!' protested Malcolm, trying to sound more polite than he felt at this intrusion.

'I know,' said the boy. 'I'm David Hick. Come and meet my dad. He's the head of all the Hicks or so he says! I'm afraid he'll want to read you Polly's letter. He sent photocopies of this amazing letter out to all our rellies back in March. That's when he persuaded most of them to come with him to this MacDonald gathering. He'd seen Rex Woodburn's advertisement in the Perth newspaper. Look, here he comes now!'

The boy laughed. His father was approaching, his arms full of papers, his face shining with exactly the same kind of enthusiasm as Uncle Don's.

'Are you from Allan's family?' the boy's father asked Malcolm, his voice breaking with excitement.

Malcolm nodded.

'Good! Come and listen to Polly's letter! I've been wanting to find someone from your camp to bridge the gap. You could take these copies to all the rest of your family for me. I don't quite like to do it myself. But sit down and listen to it first.'

Malcolm glanced at Jo. If she was willing to stay and listen, he'd stay too. Jo had no hesitation. She sat on the nearest rug and looked up at this unknown man.

'Read away!' she commanded. Malcolm sat beside her.

'Have some tea!' said the boy, handing them each a steaming mug. 'You'll need it!'

But the man's enthusiasm had waned all of a sudden. He seemed strangely reluctant to begin. He dumped his papers in a pile on the grass and selected a few pages. He shuffled them awkwardly and cleared his throat. He cleared it again.

'Go on, Dad!' said the boy.

The man tried to explain himself, still rather hesitantly. 'This is Polly Hick's story, you see,' he said, looking straight at Jo and then at Malcolm. 'I came across it only a few years ago, as a matter of fact. A lawyer in Broome put an advertisement in the local newspaper, asking for any descendants of Tom and Polly Hick to get in touch with him. I'm the only one in our family who still lives up that way so I went along to his office and he gave me this. Polly was our ancestor. She wrote this letter on a cattle station called Fairlie Bend in the far north-west of Western Australia. She put the date on it. Look! The thirty-first of January eighteen ninety-eight. Now, listen!'

The man's voice took on a new strength as he began to read.

My dear husband, Tom Hick, died a week ago today. We have buried him near the river that he loved so much. The river that saved his life. While the disturbing events of the past few months are still fresh in my mind, I want to write down all I can remember. This story will not be for my own children to read and not for their children either but in good time their grandchildren or their great-grandchildren might like to read it.

My own six dear children are still so young to be left without a father. The eldest is eighteen but the youngest is only four. I thank God that every one of them is strong and healthy. They will all have good memories of their father. I do not want them ever to be distressed by the strange things I must write in this paper. I shall send it under seal to Mr Edward Collins at the solicitor's office in Broome with strict instructions that no one is to open it for at least ninety years. That should be long enough. At any time after January 1988, the solicitor's office to which Mr Collins now belongs, or whatever firm has taken over the office by that time, will be free to seek out the descendants of any of our children to let them read this paper. I want them to know the truth about my dear Tom but I do not want anyone to know it too soon. That might only cause pain and heartbreak to them and perhaps to others if the story should spread far and wide. In ninety years from now, the truth can surely harm no one.

'I hope she's right about that!' said the man, looking up at Jo and Malcolm, his forehead furrowed with some new anxiety.

'Of course she's right,' said Jo. 'Go on!' The man went on.

I was the first of our family to set eyes on Tom. That was back in 1876 when I was twenty years old. It was a hot dry day at Fairlie Bend with a strong wind blowing clouds of sand in from the desert. We were used to days like that. My mother and sister had gone south for a few months to stay with friends. Mother was not well and we hoped that the cooler climate might help her, as indeed it did. I had stayed on at the homestead to cook the meals, to look after my father and to help the stockmen with the cattle. I was resting on the veranda at the end of the afternoon when Lily, one of the women from the blacks' camp by the river, called out to me. Her voice was urgent and frightened.

'Come, Missy. Whitefella plenty sick. Come quick, Missy.'

I hurried after her as she ran down the long slope to the river. The man lay half in the water, half out. He was naked except for a scrap of dirty cloth tied around his waist. His hands and knees were cut and bleeding as if he had crawled for miles through the rough scrubland. He was lapping at the water like a crazy dog and groaning out loud with every gulp of water that went down his throat.

'Is he really a white man, Lily?' I asked her in astonishment.

Lily nodded. She bent down and scooped up a handful of water and sand. She rubbed a patch of the man's leg until I saw the paler skin shining through the dirt.

'Who is he?' I asked.

She shook her head. 'Whitefella plenty sick,' was all she said.

I sent her off at once for my father and two of the stockmen. They carried him to the homestead and lowered him on to a bed I had made up quickly on the side veranda. I covered him with a blanket. I put water in an enamel jug, together with a mug, on a low table by the bed. The man would sleep for hours, waking up suddenly now and then and calling out in words I could not understand. I held the mug to his lips. When he had drunk, he slept again.

My father often stood at the man's bedside and gazed down at him. We agreed between us that there was no hope of bringing a doctor out so far to see him. We were two hundred miles inland from the nearest town and a hundred miles from our nearest neighbour.

'I think he'll die, Polly,' my father said many times.

I thought so too but I was sure we had to look after him as well as we could and give him a decent burial at the end.

A week after we found him, the man sat up for the first time. He made signs to me that he wanted to eat. I brought him soup and I spooned it into his mouth. I gave him bread and he gnawed at the crusts like an animal. Bit by bit his strength came back. As soon as he could manage to walk, my father led him to the river and scrubbed him clean with a rough brush and a cake of yellow soap. The man looked utterly different when he came back again, dressed in an old set of my father's clothes. I couldn't help laughing. He still didn't speak to us, at least not in English. He often mumbled a few words in some strange foreign language but they meant nothing to us.

My father tried to find out his name. He would get Lily and me to stand in front of the man and he would point to us each in turn.

'This is Lily,' my father would say loudly. 'And this is my daughter Polly. And I am Jim. Jim Hick of Fairlie Bend.'

Then he would jab his finger at the man's chest and ask him, 'What's your name, mate?'

But the man just shook his head. In the end my father simply had to give him a name.

'We'll call him Tom,' he said. 'Tom will do well enough until he remembers who he really is. When he's stronger he can help us with the cattle. I'll be glad of another pair of hands. Even if he never learns to talk, he can surely work.'

Once he was well enough, the man moved away from our veranda and had a bed in the stockmen's sleeping quarters out the back. He came to the kitchen with the men for his meals every day. He seemed to take well to the work. Bit by bit he learnt to talk, picking up new words from the men, from my father, from my mother and sister when they came back from the south, and even from me. He strung the words together like a child to start with but gradually he sounded more his age. What was his age? I often used to wonder. His hair and beard were snowy white but his face looked quite boyish sometimes. My father's guess was that Tom was a man of about forty. We soon stopped worrying about who he was and where he had come from. He was just one of the men and my father liked him.

I liked him too. I think I had always liked him from the minute I first saw him lying in the river, even though he looked so terrible then, but it took a couple of years for love to grow between us. When he told my father and mother that he wanted to marry me, they were shocked, even though they liked him. They did not really want me to marry this unknown man from nowhere but in the end they agreed. Tom had no surname so my father said he should take mine. Tom Hick he became on 20 December 1879, when the Methodist minister rode out two hundred miles from the coastal township to marry us. Our wedding took place on the front veranda with my parents, my sister, and all the stockmen and the blacks as congregation. That night Tom moved out of the men's quarters and into my bedroom in the homestead.

It was a good marriage. We were happy together. Tom soon became my father's right-hand man. As my father grew older, Tom took on more and more of the work. As my mother grew frailer and when my sister had gone south to marry, I ran the whole household and taught our children to read and write as best I could. Tom spoke English easily now. No one would have known he had not learnt it as a child. But the memories of the time before he staggered into our river never came back to him. I kept on asking him where he had been born and when he had arrived in the Colonies and what he had been doing in the desert. It was all a blank in his mind as if a dark curtain had come down on the past. Every now and then he would call out in his sleep in a strange language. I decided he must be some kind of foreigner, not English or Scottish like most people in our Western Colony. The language he spoke in his sleep sounded so peculiar to me that I thought perhaps he was a Hungarian. Hungary was the most foreign country I could think of! A country I knew nothing about.

Then six months ago, in July 1897, an odd thing happened. We were all eating our midday meal in the big kitchen together – my elderly parents, our children and the stockmen who always ate with us. Tom was at the head of the table and I was at the foot. That day there were two strangers sharing our dinner. Two men who had arrived early in the morning from somewhere further north with swags on their back. They were looking for work, they said, but we had no work to give them. Tom made them welcome and said they could stay a couple of nights in the men's quarters before they headed for the coast. There'd be plenty of work for them in the township, he told them.

Towards the end of the meal, one of the newcomers turned to the other and spoke a few fast words in a strange tongue. The other replied in similar mysterious words. I was surprised. Up until that moment both the men had spoken to us and to each other in a very pleasant musical kind of English. I had never suspected they were foreign. I was just about to ask them where in the world they came from when, to my astonishment, Tom addressed them from the head of the table. He spoke to them not in English but in some language quite unknown to me. His voice was sharp and hard. The two men were startled. They looked at each other and then one of them replied to Tom, still in this language of their own. Tom spoke to them again, more gently this time. He and the men kept up their talk for ten minutes or so, sometimes having a little trouble understanding each other but always grasping what was being said when it was repeated more slowly. The rest of us sat in silence, our eyes fixed first on Tom and then on the two men as the conversation moved back and forth between them. I was certain these visitors must be Hungarian and I was just going to say so when Tom rose from his place and the meal had ended. He followed them out to the men's quarters and spent all the rest of the day there, talking and talking. I looked in once or twice but he did not seem to see me standing at the door so I slipped away again.

'Are those two men Hungarians?' I asked Tom that night when at last he came to bed.

He laughed out loud. 'Whatever makes you think that, Polly? They're certainly not Hungarian! They're from County Donegal in Ireland. That's the Irish language they're speaking. The Irish Gaelic.'

In my ignorance I had never even heard of an Irish language. We were all English in our family and that was the only language we knew anything about.

I looked at Tom in the candlelight.

'So you must be Irish too, Tom!' I cried, the mystery solved at last. 'You were speaking to those men in their very own tongue!'

He laughed again, throwing his white head back on to the pillow. 'No, Polly, love. I'm not Irish at all. They tell me I'm not. But I do seem to know a language very like their language. Just what it is, I'm not quite sure yet, but I could understand them well enough and they could understand me. Something is stirring in my memory, Polly. Something is coming back to me from the past.'

I left it at that. I asked no more questions.

A week later Tom sat up in bed early in the morning and spoke just one word.

'Morag!' he cried, his voice breaking in grief and longing.

I had never heard the word before. He said it again and again with tears in his eyes.

'What is Morag?' I begged him. 'Where is it? How can we find it for you?'

'Morag is my sister!' he said at last. 'My beloved sister!'

That was just the beginning. Day after day new memories came flooding back to him. Soon I knew that Donald MacDonald was his father and Effie was his mother. His own name, or so he said, was Allan MacDonald. Then I heard about his other sister, Flora, and his little cousin Katie. Then he came to Kenny, his brother. But Morag was the name he spoke most often. Morag, his beloved sister.

A month later, Tom began to tell me about the Isle of Skye. Now I knew for the first time where he had come from. He was not Hungarian, after all! He was Scottish and the language he spoke, or so he said, was Gaelic from the Isle of Skye, near enough to the Irish Gaelic for him to talk with those two men. He spoke about the Isle of Skye as if it was heaven on earth. Then one day he began to talk about the sailing ship that had brought his family to the Colony of Victoria and then about a sheep-run where they had worked for years as shepherds and servants. At long last, as I had feared all along, he came to his wife. Kirsty Gordon Nicolson, his wife. His dearest wife, as he always called her. Tom could never remember how he had come to leave her but he spoke of her and of each of their children with such love and tenderness – of Allan, the eldest, named for himself as he said so proudly, then Neil and Calum and little Morag, named for his sister, and then Nicol and Gordon. Five sons and one daughter.

I was heart-broken. To discover that I had married this man Tom, or Allan MacDonald as he now called himself, when he already had a good wife and six fine children he knew not where, perhaps thousands of miles away, all still alive and well as far as we knew. It was a terrible discovery. I kept it from my parents and

I kept it from my children. They will never know. I will never tell a soul.

'I must find them, Polly,' Tom said to me urgently, day after day, 'somehow I must find them.' But I always shook my head. Better for poor Kirsty to think her Allan dead than to hear he was living with a new wife and a new set of children in the far north-west corner of Western Australia. She had had enough to suffer without that.

It was then that Tom began to sicken. Every morning he was weaker. He could not eat. He could not lift his head from the pillow. A hard dry cough racked his whole body. He was slipping away. I brought the children to say goodbye to him, one by one, and then I sat alone at his bedside for the last long night.

'Thank you, Polly,' he murmured again and again.

At six in the morning, just as the sun of a new day was bursting in through the window, he spoke for the last time.

'Kirsty, my dearest wife!' he whispered. 'Morag, my beloved sister! Where have you gone?'

And with that he died.

I decided, then and there, that the name of Allan MacDonald must die with him, at least until ninety years had passed. Then the whole world can know if it wants to. Meanwhile I mourn for him as my dear husband, Tom Hick of Fairlie Bend, father of my six children – of Jim and Mary, Margaret and Anne, William and John. I hope their descendants will think I have made the right decision when they discover it one day. I pray that the descendants of Tom's other wife, Kirsty Gordon Nicolson, will not hold anything against me if they ever happen to hear this terrible tale. May they forgive me if I have done wrong.

Tom never remembered anything about why he was in the Sandy Desert or how long he had been there or how he had managed to survive or what had finally brought him to our river in a state of exhaustion. I can only think that the Aborigines must have taken good care of him and led him to water and food. They are *the only people who know how to live in that desert. Whatever they did for him, he had forgotten it all but I am grateful.*

Signed this thirty-first day of January, 1898.

Mary (Polly) Hick.

Silence fell when the man had finished reading.

'Well!' Jo said at last. 'Allan the bigamist! That's a bit of a bombshell for a respectable family like yours, Mal! But what a good story!'

'He wasn't really a bigamist,' Malcolm said quickly, wanting to defend his ancestor. 'He'd lost his memory so he didn't have any idea what he was doing.'

'The law's the law,' Jo said with a laugh. 'I'm sure that's what your dad would say!'

'What *we* want to know,' David Hick broke in, 'is how our old Tom ever got into the desert in the first place.'

'*We* can tell you that!' Malcolm said slowly, thrusting one hand deep into his pocket. He pulled out Morag's sad letter and passed it over to David Hick who spread it on the grass and began to read, his father crouched beside him. Now Malcolm turned to Jo, taking the lead.

'Let's find my Uncle Don straight away,' he said, 'and we'll break the news. Once he's over the first terrible shock we'll bring him over to this side of the fence so he can meet all these new rellies that he never knew he had.'

'Your family cat's out of the bag all right,' Jo said with a triumphant laugh as the two of them, hand in hand, ducked under the boundary fence again and raced across the narrow strip of grass that lay between Allan's separate family circles, the Hicks and the MacDonalds.

7

Uncovering the Past

Eileen had left Morag's comfortable group behind her now and was moving purposefully towards Allan's clan. Somehow she had to find that boy. The boy in danger. She had to warn him. But warn him of what? She had no idea but at least she could find him. She approached a friendly, red-headed girl on the edge of Allan's crowd.

'Have you seen the Scottish boy?' she asked. 'I thought he'd be somewhere here. Doesn't he belong to Allan's family?'

'Malkie?' said the girl with a tinge of disappointment in her voice. 'Yes, he does belong in this family. His dad and my dad are brothers. He *was* here talking to me just a few minutes ago but now he's gone off with Jo Woodburn. He seems to like that girl much more than I do. They went right outside the white fence behind our family so they could be anywhere by now. Don't you know Jo Woodburn?'

Eileen shook her head.

'She's the daughter of that enormous Rex who gave all the announcements through the microphone,' said the girl. 'She's fourteen and she's tall and skinny and she's got untidy white hair. Her right arm's in a tartan sling. You can't miss her.'

'*White* hair!' Eileen gasped. 'But you said she was only fourteen.'

'No, not really white,' the girl laughed easily. 'But her hair's so very fair it does *look* white when the sun shines on it. It's untidy hair. It sticks up all over her head. My mum says it could do with a good thorough brush.'

'So where should I look next?' Eileen asked. 'I've just come from Morag's crowd. He wasn't there.'

'You could try Katie's lot,' the girl suggested. 'That's the next group round the edge of the oval. See, over there, just past the goalposts. Then you could go on to Kenny's family and end up at Flora's. If he comes back here I'll be sure to tell him you're looking for him.'

'Thanks,' Eileen said. 'Tell him it's urgent!'

'Urgent!' Chloë murmured in surprise when Eileen had run off towards Katie's blue flag.

Almost everyone in Katie's family was in a state of high indignation.

'Did you hear what that Woodburn fellow was saying about our Katie?' one tall man was fuming to anyone who would listen, his face red with anger, his hands trembling. 'Only a cousin!'

'And an orphan! Found in Greenock! It's disgusting!' said the woman standing next to him.

'We'll show him the Bible!' said the red-faced man. 'That'll settle the question once and for all.'

'Whatever's the matter?' Eileen asked a girl about her own age in the middle of Katie's seething crowd.

The girl smiled at her. 'They're all terribly upset,' she said quietly. 'That organizer who was shouting through the microphone – you know, Rex Woodburn in the funny kilt – he said our Katie was only an orphan cousin. But everyone in our family is sure she was really the youngest sister. As if it matters! I don't mind what she was. My rellies take these things far too seriously.'

'What's the Bible he's talking about?'

'Our Katie inherited the family Bible. Didn't you know? It's just over here on the table. I'll show you. Come on.'

Eileen picked up the small black book and turned the pages. She couldn't understand a word of it. That strange language must be Gaelic, just as Mum had predicted.

'Look at this bit that Katie wrote in the front,' said the girl. 'Our family loves this page best. It's in English, for one thing. We used to have it recited to us when we were little children, along with all the usual nursery rhymes and fairy tales.'

Eileen read the words, written in a spidery hand, inside the front cover of the Bible.

My name is Catriona Matheson but I am always called Katie. I was born Catriona MacDonald on the Isle of Skye in April, 1852, the youngest child of Donald and Effie MacDonald. My brothers were Allan and Kenny; my sisters were Morag and Flora. I sailed to Australia with my family when I was only a few months old. Our ship was the Georgiana *but I remember nothing of the voyage and nothing of our first few years in the Colony. When I grew up I married Murdo Matheson. He had come from the Isle of Skye as a baby on the very same ship as our own family. Murdo and I had twelve dear children. He died on 22 June last year, 1920, at the age of sixty-eight. He is buried in the family grave at Linton.*

When my mother, Effie MacDonald, lay dying in 1882, she put this Bible into my hands. She wanted me to have it, whatever the others might say – and they did have plenty to say! Today I am passing it on to my youngest daughter, Mairi. Please keep it safe in our family from one generation

to the next. Let the youngest always be the one to have it.
Our children and grandchildren have lost the old Skye
language but surely it will do them good to hold in their
hands this Gaelic Bible that my parents loved to read every
day of their lives.
   Katie Matheson, 15 September 1921.

'See!' said the angry man, rushing up to the table where
Eileen and the girl were bent over the Bible. 'It says there,
as plain as day, that Katie was the youngest child of Effie
and Donald MacDonald! I'm going to show Rex Woodburn that he's talking through his hat!'

'His glengarry bonnet,' Eileen corrected him gently.

'Bonnet! Hat! Whatever the ridiculous thing is! There
are Katie's words in black ink!'

'But those words only tell us what Katie *believed* about
herself,' Eileen said, hoping it wasn't too rude to argue
back. 'She simply wrote down what Donald and Effie had
told her. The older children in the family might have
known a completely different story. They might have
remembered she was only a cousin.'

The man stared at Eileen, annoyed and puzzled.

'But if our Katie wrote it in her Bible, it *must* be true!'
he said. 'No one would write lies in a Bible!'

'She *thought* it was true. Why don't you ask Rex why
he thinks she was an orphan cousin? Ask him for some
proof.'

'That's exactly what I'm going to do!' cried the man,
snatching up the Bible and storming off to find Rex
Woodburn.

When Eileen was sure that Malcolm was not lurking
anywhere in Katie's family, she ran over to Kenny's flag
where she hovered on the edge of every chattering circle,
listening to scraps of conversation, her eyes searching all

the time for the elusive boy and for the girl with white hair. They were definitely not there. She couldn't resist pausing for a few minutes to look at the splendid array of family heirlooms set out on Kenny's table. Old brown photographs, old frayed maps, old letters, old marriage certificates, old school report books, a lacy wedding dress, a horse's collar, a baby's tiny bonnet and a handful of small white pebbles.

'Where do these pebbles come from?' she asked the nearest boy, trickling them through her fingers.

'No idea,' he said pleasantly, shrugging his shoulders. 'Are you some kind of relly of mine?'

Eileen nodded. 'I'm Eileen Gallagher from Morag's family,' she said. 'I'm trying to find that Scottish boy.'

The boy shrugged again. Eileen ran on at once to Flora's flag where the angry man from Katie's family was already confronting Rex Woodburn with the words written so plainly in the Gaelic Bible. Rex was retaliating as tactfully as he could with a photocopied record of all the baptisms and deaths in some Greenock parish in 1852. Eileen came closer to look. There was the clear evidence that Catriona MacDonald had been born in Greenock to Iain and Silis MacDonald on 10 April in that year. There were the deaths of poor Silis herself in May and then of Iain in July. The parish minister had written beside Katie's name: *This orphaned infant emigrated to Australia with cousins from the Isle of Skye on the* Georgiana, *13 July 1852.* The red-faced man retreated, quite crestfallen. Eileen watched him making his way slowly back to Katie's group, the Bible clenched in one hand and the Greenock parish records in the other. He was clearly not looking forward to the task of breaking such unwelcome news to the rest of his family. Eileen turned away. She felt sorry for the man. In any case, the Scottish boy was not here. She rushed back to Morag's family where she knew she'd feel more at home. Perhaps Malcolm MacDonald had been there all the time.

'Eileen!' a familiar voice called out to her. It was Bob MacRae with Gill beside him. They both seemed so pleased to have found her again.

'We've been looking for that Scottish boy,' Bob said.

'So have I,' said Eileen.

'The trouble is,' said Bob, 'he seems to keep moving round from one part of this gathering to the next. As soon as we reach one group we're told he's gone! We're on our way to Allan's flag now. That's where he really belongs so perhaps we'll run him to earth this time. All we want with him is a friendly chat.'

'He's not there, Bob,' Eileen said. 'Or he wasn't a little while ago. I can't find him anywhere.'

'Well, let's try Allan's lot again,' said Bob, taking Eileen by the arm. 'He might've come back there by now.'

As the three of them moved nearer to Allan's flag they stopped and stared. This whole family was in utter turmoil. Yellow flags were being brandished among the blue. Irate relations clearly labelled 'Hick' or 'MacDonald' were confronting each other with pale faces. Papers were being passed from hand to hand. Some people were crying. Others were shouting. A few of the younger ones were even laughing.

'What on earth's going on?' Eileen asked the same red-haired girl she'd seen last time.

'Bigamy!' said the girl, her green eyes flashing with excitement. 'Who would've thought we'd come across anything like that in our dull old family? It seems that our Allan MacDonald left his family just for one year, or so he thought, to go on some mad expedition right through the heart of the Australian desert. He never came back. His wife and children assumed he was dead. But we've just discovered that a few years later he staggered out of the desert somewhere over in Western Australia. He'd completely lost his memory. He didn't know who he was. He couldn't even speak English any more. To cut a long story short, he married a girl called Polly Hick, he took her name and they had six children. Dozens of their descendants are here today. We'd never heard of them before. It's amazing!'

'Some of your older folk seem really distressed,' said Gill in concern, looking around at the tear-stained faces.

'Yes, they are,' the girl admitted. 'They feel it's a terrible blot on our family's good name. But honestly, those Hicks from the west are such nice people. We've got so much in common with them. They even *look* like us! Still, it must've been very hard for Allan's wife Kirsty. She was left to earn her living as housekeeper to some poor widower and she had to bring up his children along with hers. *She's* the one we all want to know more about now but almost everything about her seems to have been lost or forgotten. No diaries, no letters, no old stories, nothing! She's the invisible woman!'

'Every family has them,' said Gill.

'Did that Scottish boy ever come back here?' Eileen asked the girl.

'Yes, he did!' she laughed. 'He's the one who brought us the amazing news about Allan's second family. He and Jo found all these Hicks just over the fence. But he's gone again now. I'm Chloë MacDonald, by the way. Who are you?'

'Eileen Gallagher from up in the Mallee,' Eileen said with a smile. 'And this is Bob and Gill MacRae from Tasmania. We're all from the same family. Morag's family.'

'Morag's family!' Chloë exclaimed, her eyes lighting up. 'She was always so close to our old Allan, you know. And

85

she was the one who was supposed to have the second sight.'

'I know,' Eileen said, a shiver creeping to the back of her neck as she remembered.

'I don't believe a word of it, of course, but Malkie says it could be true. He says it's sometimes passed down from one generation of a family to the next.'

Eileen nodded. 'I know,' she said again, determined not to give too much away.

'You're sure to find Malkie at the dance tonight, anyway,' Chloë said cheerfully. 'And if you don't see him there, look out for him at the church tomorrow morning. Rex wants him to read something in the service so you won't be able to miss him. I did tell him you were looking for him. I told him it was urgent too but Jo just grabbed his hand again and they ran off together without a care in the world.'

Eileen thought Chloë looked rather sad in spite of her happy voice and her confident manner.

'Do you like him?' she asked Chloë directly. 'This Scottish boy?'

'Yes, I do. He's a bit shy and awkward but I think he's toughening up already. Mum says all he really needs is a good long stay in Australia and then he'd be as right as rain but he has to go back to Scotland at the end of next week.'

'Well, thanks, Chloë. Do tell him again that I'm –'

'Looking for him!' Chloë broke in with a smile. 'I'll tell him.' She moved away.

'Let's go back to our own Morag's family,' Bob said, his old brown face creased with weariness. 'I'm getting confused among so many strangers.'

Eileen was as glad as Bob and Gill to be among more familiar faces again. She had something to tell her mother.

'I've seen that Gaelic Bible, Mum,' she shouted excitedly, the minute they came face to face again at the heart of Morag's family. 'Katie had it!'

'Katie!' exclaimed Mum in surprise and with a touch of indignation. 'Why didn't Effie leave it to Allan? He was the eldest!'

'I'll tell you why!' exclaimed Eileen, jubilant at the prospect of spilling the beans about Allan's disappearance and then the double family.

Bob and Gill didn't wait to hear the story again. They wandered off to the very edge of Morag's group and sat down together on the grass, their backs to the whole happy crowd.

At eight o'clock on Sunday morning, a long fleet of cars and buses left the centre of Geelong and took the road for Linton. The party on Saturday night had been a great success in two adjacent halls, both of them decorated with gaudy balloons and streamers. Dancing, singing, eating, drinking and endless talking. Eileen had enjoyed herself well enough with all her new relations but she still felt unsettled. At the back of her mind was an awkward sense of urgency that made her move restlessly from one hall to the other. She'd certainly caught a glimpse of that quiet, dark-haired boy on the far side of the crowd more than once. Every time she saw him he was standing close to a thin girl whose arm was hoisted up across her chest in a tartan sling, but whenever Eileen came any nearer, the pair of them seemed to melt away into the throng. In the end, when the party had ended at midnight, there was nothing she could do but leave her search till the next day at the country church. She comforted herself with the thought that she could easily find Chloë again there. Chloë stood out plainly in any crowd. Chloë would lead her to Malcolm.

Eileen's family was among the last to reach the little weatherboard church a few miles beyond Linton. By that time the large congregation had completely filled the building and was overflowing into the garden where people sat on rugs spread out on the grass. Rex Woodburn had thought of everything. Loudspeakers were hanging from all the wattle trees around the church so everyone could hear what was going on inside. Eileen found a slender sapling to lean against and joined in the first hymn as best she could, though she didn't recognize the words or the tune. It amused her to see all these people singing away so heartily in the open air, shielding their eyes against the glare of the sun. It was the strangest kind of church service she had ever been to.

'And now,' said the minister from inside the church, 'our young visitor from Scotland, Malcolm MacDonald, will read to us from Psalm Thirty-four.'

Eileen could tell that the boy was nervous as soon as she heard his voice. He gulped before he began and even stuttered slightly on the first few words.

'I will b-bless the Lord at all t-times,' he read carefully.

By the fourth verse he had gathered confidence and the stutter had gone.

'I sought the Lord and he heard me,' he declared boldly, his soft Scottish voice floating down from the trees. Eileen was distracted for an instant by a long black ant climbing on to her sandals. She shook her foot to toss the ant off. Then she caught the boy's voice again.

'O taste and see that the Lord is good,' he read. 'Blessed is the man that trusteth in him.'

Eileen gasped. 'O taste and see!' she exclaimed out loud. 'That's exactly what old Morag said to me!'

'Shh!' hissed a chorus of irate cousins sitting near by, waving flies away from their faces.

Eileen was silent. She hardly heard the rest of the service. The long sermon passed her by completely. She kept thinking about the Scottish boy. It was uncanny that he'd read those very words that Morag had spoken to her under the fennel. 'O taste and see!' Morag's voice came sharply back to her memory. 'Keep close to him then!'

The minute the minister's booming benediction had brought the service to its end, Eileen began to move forward, watching and waiting for those inside the church to come out again.

'Buses leave in five minutes!' Rex Woodburn roared cheerfully through the loudspeakers. 'Hurry up, everyone. All aboard for Brolga Marsh!'

That was the moment when she saw him. Or rather she saw the girl first. A skinny girl with a thatch of spiky white hair. The girl was gripping the boy's elbow with her left hand. Eileen raced towards them, pushing her way roughly through the crowd, coming nearer and nearer as they climbed on to the second last bus.

'Malcolm!' she called. 'Wait for me!'

She was too late. The door closed, the engine purred, the bus moved off. She could see Malcolm's puzzled face looking back at her through the window. She waved. He waved and was gone.

Chloë was beside her in an instant.

'Missed him again?' she asked with a grin. 'No worries. Come with me in my dad's car and we'll easily catch him up at Brolga Marsh.'

'Thanks,' said Eileen, trying to smother her disappointment.

In the car, she met Chloë's parents. She liked them at

once in that same odd, instinctive way that she'd liked a few people in all the other families.

'What exactly is this house we're going to?' she asked. 'Mum did tell me which house is which but I've forgotten now. She said we were seeing two of them today.'

'This one's Brolga Marsh. It's a lovely old bluestone homestead from the early days,' said Chloë's father, delighted to have a new audience for the family details he knew so well. 'It used to be owned by William Martin but I'm not sure who owns it now. Whoever it is has said we can come and see where our ancestors lived.'

'Did they actually *live* in the house?' Eileen asked him.

'No, no. That was just for the Martin family. Our folk were only the servants and the shepherds so they lived in a log hut out the back. Hasn't your mother ever passed on any tales about that little log hut? My father knew dozens of stories. Old stories and old songs.'

'I think she's tried,' laughed Eileen. 'But I wouldn't listen. Now we're actually going to see it, I wish I'd paid more attention.'

'I'm afraid we won't see the hut,' said Chloë's father. 'It must have fallen down years ago. But we'll certainly see the place where it once stood. And we might see some signs of where the Aborigines had their camp by the creek.'

'Will we see the brolgas dancing on the marsh?' Eileen asked him, not sure why she asked.

'No, they've all gone, I'm afraid. There are almost no birds left on that marsh nowadays, or so I've heard. The Aborigines have gone too, of course. My grandfather had a story about how a gang of wild, white shearers chased all those blacks off into the bush one hot summer in the eighteen seventies. They never came back again. Not surprising, the way they were treated. How did you know that the brolgas used to dance on the marsh in the early days, Eileen? Did your mother tell you?'

She shook her head, quite confused herself. 'No. Perhaps it was just the name of the place that made me think of it. Brolga Marsh. I can't remember how I know about those dancing birds but they seem as clear in my mind as if I'd actually seen them.'

The car swung between two tall stone pillars and sped up a long driveway to the house. Rex Woodburn was there already, directing cars and buses to a dry paddock for parking. The present owner of Brolga Marsh sat in a cane chair on his front veranda, waving benignly to all the people as they streamed past his garden.

'Great day you've got for it!' he called.

'Wonderful!' they called back.

Eileen followed the crowd right down to the creek. She was disappointed, even though Chloë's father had warned her not to expect too much. There really wasn't anything exciting to see. Only a few post holes showed where the family's hut had once stood and, on the very edge of the creek, lay a few scattered cutting stones and a pile of what might once have been fish bones, now disintegrating into dust. That was all that remained of the Aborigines' camp where Morag's friend Kal-Kal must have lived. Kal-Kal of the emu feathers. Eileen kicked impatiently at the dusty pile. The earth broke open at the top and uncovered a small white shell glinting in the sunlight.

Eileen picked up the shell and held it close to her ear. Could this really be the little shell from Skye that Morag said she had given to Kal-Kal? And was that the sound of the sea she could hear faintly surging in the depths of her ear? She moved quickly away from the mob of chattering relations and found a place to sit by herself, comfortably propped against the trunk of an old she-oak and close to the water. She gazed across the bubbling creek towards the thick scrub on the far bank. That might be the very place where Morag had once seen four tall Highlanders carrying a coffin. There was certainly no coffin there today. No Highlanders either. And no glimpse of Morag herself, either the bare-footed girl from the bus or the old woman under the fennel in a brown straw hat. Then, quite suddenly, she heard the singing.

May the red sun be with us wherever we go,
Over the green hills and over the sea,
Waking us early, so far from our home,
Over the green hills and over the sea.

Eileen jumped up and turned her head this way and that but she saw no singer. The voice sang on, young and clear and confident. She began to hum along with the tune. It was easy. As she hummed, she heard the words whirling around her.

May the new moon be with us wherever we go,
Over the green hills and over the sea,
Silver and shining, so far from our home,
Over the green hills and over the sea.

'Where are you?' Eileen called across the water. 'I can't see you!'

'Don't give up so soon!' a voice called back to her. 'Find the quiet boy!'

'I'm doing my best!' Eileen shouted indignantly, speaking to the empty air. 'I haven't given up but I just can't find that boy! He keeps moving on!'

'There's danger!' said the voice.

'I know! You've told me that already! But I'm beginning

to think that something's stopping me from finding the boy! I've seen him but I just can't get close to him!'

'Take the shell and try again!'

Before Eileen could make any reply, the singing started up once more. Sometimes the song came clearly from the far side of the creek, sometimes from behind her, sometimes close at hand.

> *May the fairies be with us wherever we go,*
> *Over the green hills and over the sea,*
> *Bringing us blessing, so far from our home,*
> *Over the green hills and over the sea.*

Now the song was fading.

'Come back!' Eileen bellowed, tears of real fear filling her eyes as the tune grew fainter and the words became blurred.

'Eileen! Whatever's the matter?' Bob and Gill had found her again.

'Nothing,' she mumbled and put out both her hands to touch them.

'What's that you're holding?' Gill asked, seeing a small flash of white between her fingers.

'Only some old shell. I found it.'

Eileen pushed the shell into her pocket where the sprig of fennel lay safe and secure.

'Nothing much to see here,' Bob said gloomily. 'It's hard to imagine our old Morag living in a place like this, isn't it?'

Eileen made no answer. She was unwilling to trust her voice to tell Bob that she could imagine Morag living here only too easily. The sense of Morag's presence was so strong it was almost painful. She longed to escape from its impossible demands.

'Let's get going to the next house. The family mansion

or whatever Rex Woodburn calls it!' Gill said. 'I'm feeling hungry now and that barbecue'll be ready and waiting for us when we get there. The best part of the day! Do come in our bus, Eileen. We've been missing you.'

'I think I'll go in Chloë's car again, if you don't mind. She's promised to find . . . to show me something. But I'll be sure to see you there. I'm hungry too! Desperately hungry!'

Eileen was surprised to feel this sudden hunger gripping her stomach but she was glad at the same time. There was something quite ordinary and reassuring about hunger.

The 'family mansion', as Rex always called it, was far grander than Brolga Marsh. In fact it seemed much too grand for comfort. Eileen didn't like her first view of the house from the back seat of Chloë's dad's car.

'Who lived here?' she asked as she stared at the palatial building with its symmetrical rows of windows and its imposing flight of steps up to the front door. 'Was it one of your ancestors, Chloë?'

'No! It was one of *yours*!' Chloë answered. 'Our lot never had money like that. One of Morag's sons built this place. Isn't that right, Dad?'

'Not quite,' said Chloë's father as he parked in a grassy paddock, filling up already with other cars. 'Four of Morag's sons built this place between them and somehow they all lived here together for years and years. There's plenty of room for four families, of course, but it's not my idea of happiness. I wonder if they had four separate kitchens and four dining-room tables or did they cook and eat together?'

'I suppose they had servants to do the cooking!' Chloë said. 'Where did all their money come from?'

94

'A gold mine in Bendigo, I think,' said her father. 'They struck it lucky, those four brothers.'

Eileen thought at once of 'wee Donald' and his bitter grievance against his older brothers but she didn't want to risk probing that story yet. She switched her thoughts quickly to her own ancestor Effie, Morag's eldest daughter. That would be an easier way into the past.

'Didn't the four sisters get a share in the gold mine?' she asked.

'I'm sure they did, Eileen,' said Chloë's father. 'Those four brothers would have been generous but we've never heard much about it. Your Morag's family rather lost touch with our Allan's family after he disappeared into that desert.'

'But who lives here now?' Eileen asked.

'No one – apart from the caretaker and some kind of warden. The house belongs to a Heritage Trust and it's generally only open to the public on Wednesdays and Saturdays but Rex made a special arrangement for us to see it on a Sunday. He's had permission to set up all the barbecues at one end of the orchard and he tells me he's got a whole team of local volunteers to do the grilling for us. Can't you smell it, Eileen?'

She could. She could hear Rex Woodburn too. He was nowhere to be seen but his amplified voice seemed to bounce off the sky.

'Welcome to the family mansion! You'll all have a chance to see it properly after lunch. First, we're going to eat. Just look on the front cover of your programmes to find the number of your table and then make your way to the right one. You'll see the tables set out under the trees in the orchard. We've done our best to mix you all up so you'll make friends with new people from other parts of the family. Hurry along now. The salads are made and the meat's ready. The wine's flowing and so's the beer. Just find your table, sit down and hoe in!'

'What's the number on your programme, Eileen?' Chloë asked her as they came right into the orchard where dozens of cheery men in striped aprons were tending the long rows of glowing barbecues. 'I hope we'll be together.'

Eileen fished out her forgotten programme. 'Sixteen!' she said.

'Mine's forty-five!' Chloë said with a groan. 'Dad? What about you and Mum?'

'Seven,' he said.

'I do wish we could stay together,' Chloë said. Eileen nodded. She thought Rex was mad to start breaking up all the new friendships that had only just begun.

'Couldn't we go where we like?' she suggested. 'He'd never know!'

'Oh, yes he would!' Chloë's mother laughed. 'I think we'd better follow his system. There'll be chaos if we don't.'

'There seems to be chaos anyway,' Eileen said as she gazed at the hundreds of bewildered people wandering up and down under the apple trees, all of them searching for the right table with the right number. Bit by bit, a kind of order did begin to emerge from all the confusion.

'There's table sixteen, Eileen!' cried Chloë, pointing.

Eileen sank thankfully into a chair as the others moved on. She smiled at the six people already sitting around the table. They smiled back at her with friendly faces but no one spoke. She wondered who would be coming to fill the last empty seat, right next to her own.

And then she saw him! The Scottish boy himself! He was walking slowly towards table sixteen. His dark eyes seemed anxious as he parted from the thin girl with the tartan sling. He kept watching the girl as she turned away in a new direction. Then he checked the number on his programme and put one hesitant hand on the back of the empty chair.

'Hullo, Malcolm!' Eileen cried in delight. 'I've been looking for you everywhere!'

'Who *are* you?' he asked in surprise, sitting down beside her.

'I'm Eileen Gallagher from Morag's family,' she said and then lowered her voice. 'Malcolm! There's something I have to tell you! Something very important!'

'Whatever is it?' he asked, startled at her intensity.

Eileen leant closer towards him. 'There's danger!' she whispered.

Malcolm stared at her in astonishment. Then he threw back his head and laughed out loud.

'Danger!' he cried, not bothering to drop his voice to match hers. 'Danger in the heart of our wonderful family! You must be joking!'

8

Safe and Secure

Eileen had no idea how to get Malcolm to take her warning seriously. Since she couldn't even guess herself what the terrible danger might be, she could hardly convince him of it. She glanced around at the circle of silent relatives, all of them waiting patiently for their meal, none of them quite knowing what to say to anyone else. Obviously, they were feeling uneasy and even a bit resentful, torn away from the closer families they'd met already. At that very moment, two of the aproned men who'd been grilling steaks and baking potatoes on the barbecues approached the table with cheerful grins and began to serve. Eileen jumped up and pushed the salad bowl politely towards each cousin in turn until every plate was heaped high. Malcolm followed her lead and began to pour wine, beer or orange juice into every glass.

'Now we can start!' Eileen announced, smiling around at the timid faces to give them encouragement. At last the tongues were loosened and, as the eating began, everyone at the table turned to someone else, introduced themselves, explained which branch of the family they belonged to, told where they lived and how they had heard about this extraordinary gathering in the first place, passed on various

versions of old family stories. The whole table buzzed with
easy talk and laughter.

'I am the Witch-Cat!' one dear old lady shrieked out
loud to her neighbour. Whatever could she mean? Eileen
wondered in astonishment.

'Just keep filling up their glasses!' she murmured to
Malcolm.

He nodded obediently and gave a quick sideways look
at this rather bossy cousin of his who seemed to have taken
charge of the whole table. This Eileen Gallagher. She
looked reasonably all right, he thought. Fair hair, a scattering of freckles, a good smile, the family look. But the
trouble was, as he realized with the stab of a new and
painful sensation somewhere inside his chest, she was
nothing at all like Jo! Jo had gone off to sit with a bunch
of strangers at some other table. How could he pretend
to take any interest in this unknown and ordinary girl,
Eileen Gallagher, with her peculiar warnings about danger
when the only thing he wanted was to find Jo again? This
Eileen wasn't startling or remarkable or exciting in any
way. Jo was absolutely startling. He had never met anyone
like her in his whole life. Just knowing her seemed to
make him feel quite different. Older, taller, more confident, cleverer.

Malcolm shifted about restlessly in his seat, looking first
over one shoulder and then over the other, hoping to
catch sight of Jo somewhere among the hundreds of
people who were gathered around their tables in the
orchard. He couldn't see her at all. The whole day seemed
grey and pointless and he wished he'd never come to
Australia. He should have stayed at home in Scotland.
Suddenly, with an unexpected lurch of memory, he
thought of Fiona for the first time in three days. He slid
his hand into his pocket to make sure the penny whistle

she'd given him was still there. He pulled it out and put it on the table, close to his plate. That made him feel safer, somehow.

Eileen's eyes lit up at once. Perhaps she could get this silent boy talking at last.

'Can you play tunes on your tin whistle?' she asked him.

'I'm just beginning to get the hang of it,' he said cautiously. 'I used to play a recorder in primary school and this is not so very different. Want a go?'

'Thanks.'

Eileen took the whistle, wiped her mouth, and began to play a sad Scottish tune that her mother always liked to hum to herself as she pegged the washing on the line in a hot northerly wind. The six other people at the table looked up at her with puzzled faces.

' "Ye Banks and Braes"!' exclaimed Malcolm, recognizing the song at once. 'You play really well. Have you got one of these whistles yourself?'

She nodded. 'It's Dad's really, but he lets me play it.' She passed the whistle back to him.

'Tell me all about your school, Malcolm,' Eileen demanded pleasantly now that the ice was broken. She had decided to leave any more warnings about danger until this boy had loosened up a bit. 'I have to give a talk to my class when we get back home. A talk about this gathering and the different people we've met here. I suppose you'll be doing the same thing when you get back to Scotland.'

Malcolm gaped at her in amazement.

'Never!' he said. 'I'll be working hard to catch up on all the stuff I've missed.'

'Didn't you *want* to come to Australia?'

Malcolm was astonished at how quickly this girl went straight to the heart of things.

'Not really,' he admitted. 'It was Dad's idea. He wanted me to be here. But it's turned out much better than I expected. I wouldn't have met Jo Woodburn if I hadn't come. She's an amazing cousin. You must meet her, Eileen.'

Eileen nodded but she steered him back to talking about school. That might lead on to something more personal. If he would only talk about himself she might be nearer to guessing just what the danger could be.

'What's your favourite subject?' she asked him.

'French,' he said promptly, 'but I like science too. I want to be a vet.'

'A vet in France?' she asked him, puzzled.

'No,' he laughed quietly, relaxing a little more with every minute. 'I want to be a vet in Scotland but we do go to France for our holidays when we don't head north to Skye. Dad's crazy about Skye but Mum loves France. Where do you have your holidays?'

It was the first time Malcolm had managed to ask her anything. Eileen felt triumphant. She was getting him started at last.

'Nowhere!' she said with a laugh. 'My dad's a wheat farmer up in the Mallee. That's in north-west Victoria. Hot and dry. Farmers never like taking holidays. They always say too much can go wrong on the farm while they're away, even when one of the neighbours is keeping an eye on things. We were lucky that Dad agreed to take this whole week off for the family gathering. Usually we just stay at home for our holidays. I read books and swim in the pool and help Dad on the farm. Sometimes I go camping for a few nights with my brothers. Up in the Sunset Country. It's great up there. I love it. Do you go camping in Scotland?'

'Not in Scotland,' Malcolm said with a shiver as he

remembered the chill of last summer. 'Mum and Dad think it's far too cold, though plenty of other people do camp there. We generally go camping in France.'

At last Eileen had found something she had in common with this boy. Camping! She plied him with a barrage of questions about camping in France until every plate at the table was clean. He answered her willingly enough but she could see that his mind was never quite on the subject. He glanced back over his shoulder yet again while Eileen was collecting the dirty plates and taking them to the nearest washing-up point. Then, as she came back to the table and began to ladle out generous helpings of fruit salad and cream, he actually stood up for a few seconds and gazed all around the orchard. She heard him groan under his breath. She made one final effort.

'I'm really looking forward to seeing over this big family mansion, aren't you?' she asked him.

'Yes,' he said politely. Eileen gave up the struggle. She decided she would just have to stick close to his side when everyone went off to see the mansion. She remembered Morag's words. 'Keep close to him.' That was the only thing she could do. Keep close. She felt in her pocket for the fennel and the shell. She gripped them tight.

'Ah, there she is at last!' Malcolm cried joyfully, leaping out of his seat and almost running towards the tall skinny girl who was striding over the grass towards him, her arm bouncing about loosely in its tartan sling. Eileen ran after him.

'This is Jo,' Malcolm said proudly. 'Jo, this is Eileen from Morag's family.'

'Hi!' Eileen said, grinning up at her.

'Hi!' said Jo without a smile and turned back to Malcolm. 'I've been stuck at the world's most boring table. I thought I'd never get away from those awful cousins.

Aren't you ready to come with me now? Andy's waiting for us.'

'Andy?' Malcolm said in surprise. 'Has he come to look over this house with us?'

Jo laughed. 'Nothing like that,' she said. 'He just wants to show us something, he says. It's around the other side of the house. Come on!'

'I'll come too,' Eileen offered.

'Don't bother,' said Jo, pleasantly enough but with a definite edge to her voice. 'Malcolm'll be fine with me. We'll come back to see that monstrosity of a house later. We're sure to find you somewhere in there.'

Eileen swung round to face Malcolm.

'Don't go!' she begged him. 'You know what I told you.'

'Sorry! I've forgotten already!' he said with a laugh, putting out one hand to grab Jo's hand.

'There's danger!' Eileen hissed at him, embarrassed at having to speak such words in front of Jo.

'Rubbish!' Jo snapped angrily. 'Malcolm's not a little boy to be tied to your apron strings. Just leave him alone! Let him do what he likes!'

'Malcolm! Please don't go!' Eileen shouted in despair. 'Or let me come with you!'

'Push off!' Malcolm answered rudely, taking Jo firmly by the arm and turning his back on Eileen. The two of them went off laughing together. Eileen's eyes were full of tears. She stood still in the orchard while the crowds at the tables chattered merrily all around her. What could she do? She couldn't tag along where she wasn't wanted. She knew she had handled the whole thing badly but it was too late to start again. At that moment Rex Woodburn's deep voice boomed down at her from the loudspeakers in the trees.

'Well, all you dear rellies, the great family mansion is now open! This is the wonderful house that Morag's four sons built for themselves back in the eighteen eighties. This is where they lived so happily together with all their children for years and years. There's nothing quite like this beautiful old house in the whole of Australia! In the whole of the *world*, as a matter of fact! We can all be proud of it! Just take your time, friends. When you've finished eating, make your way up the front steps and wander about the house wherever you like. I know you're going to love it! The buses will leave for Geelong in two hours from now so there's plenty of time. No hurries! No worries!' Rex chuckled into the microphone at the end of his speech.

Eileen made a dash for the house. She wanted to be the first up those steps. Perhaps from some high window on the far side she could look down on Malcolm, just to make sure that all was well until Jo brought him safely back again. She could surely keep an eye on him, even if she couldn't keep close to him.

The floor of the grand entrance hall was tiled in blues and greens. A welcoming fire of huge logs sparked and crackled in the hearth. An oval mirror hung over the fireplace. Wide doors stood open to left and right. Eileen could glimpse on one side a dining room with its long, polished table and a display of splendid silver. On the other side was a fine drawing room with still more rooms opening beyond it. The carpets were rich with reds and blues. The chandeliers were sparkling. She felt at once the strange pull of this place. Morag had been here.

Straight ahead of her in the hall rose a magnificent staircase of white marble. Eileen began to climb the stairs, her hand on the cool banister. Old Morag's words under the fennel bushes darted back into her mind, pushing away her fears for Malcolm. 'In the cedarwood box. At the turn of the stairs. In the fine big house. Safe and secure.' Was this the right house? Were these the right stairs? Then where was the box?

At the first turning, the dark portrait of a stern, bearded gentleman gazed down at her. One of Morag's prosperous sons perhaps? At the second turning, a stuffed lyrebird in a case fixed her with a glassy eye. She shivered. On the first-floor landing she tiptoed down the wide passageways, first to the east and then to the west, where one open door after another showed her the family bedrooms, spacious and well furnished. Velvet curtains. Heavy white bedspreads. The stairs climbed higher. Eileen went on up.

On the second floor, she dashed along each of the two corridors to see what she could find. An old-fashioned night nursery with rows of white cots. A day nursery with a rocking-horse, a doll's house and a box of toys. Then a schoolroom with desks arranged in pairs, a dusty black-board, sticks of white chalk and a table for the governess. Then on to a play room, a junk room, and a box room stuffed with tin trunks. Eileen ran back to the staircase and climbed higher still to the third floor.

These stairs were narrower. They were not made of white marble but of polished brown wood. Ten smooth steps and then a sharp turn. Ten more steps. Another turn. And then she saw it! The cedarwood box! Low and long and thrust back against the wall on the very last turning of the attic stairs. Eileen stood still and caught her breath. She bent to lift the lid. It wasn't locked. It opened easily. She peered inside and let out a cry of disappointment. The cedarwood box held nothing but a pile of thin, white blankets.

The distant buzz of voices now rose up the staircase

from far below. Eileen could hear exclamations of delight as the family mob flowed into the hallway and began to explore the dining room, the drawing rooms and even the vast kitchens down in the basement. No one was climbing the stairs yet but it wouldn't be long. She knelt by the box and took out the well-worn blankets one by one, setting them down carefully beside her in a soft, white stack on the floor. The musty smell of old wool and mothballs filled her nostrils. She sneezed. She leant back on her heels and gazed down into the empty box.

'Nothing!' she said in a sad, bleak voice.

Quickly her fingers searched the lining of the box for hidden panels, secret pouches, false bottoms. Nothing like that at all. It was just an empty box, solid and strong, looking and smelling as if no one had bothered to open it for years. These old blankets were far too thin to give any sleeper much warmth in winter. Eileen got to her feet again and took hold of the blanket at the top of her pile. She grasped it firmly by two corners and shook it vigorously. Then she folded it back into the box. She did the same with the second blanket and then seized the third, her exasperation growing. As she gave it a good shake, something fell to the floor. Eileen's heart leapt to her mouth as she scooped up a thin exercise book with a shiny black cover.

'Safe and secure!' she murmured as she flicked through the pages. Neat old-fashioned handwriting in careful straight lines. She read the words at the head of each page out loud, but not too loud.

'Kangaroo Tail Soup. River-Fish Baked in Mud (Kal-Kal taught me this). Roast Snake. Feathered Birds Cooked in Clay and Hot Ashes. Digger's Damper. Early Settlers' Cake. Scripture Cake . . . Take four and a half cupfuls of first Kings, chapter four, verse twenty-two; one and a half cupfuls of Judges, chapter five, verse twenty-five; two cupfuls of Jeremiah, chapter six, verse twenty . . .'

Eileen laughed and turned back to the first page of the book. There, as plain as day, was the name she was longing to find. *Morag MacDonald, Brolga Marsh, 1858.*

Morag's recipe book! But what use would these old recipes be in warning Malcolm of some unknown danger? And how could roast snakes and scripture cakes sort out the cheating of poor wee Donald? If Morag really wanted this book to be found, why did she leave it in a box where no one was likely to look? The whole thing was hopeless.

Eileen listened. The excited crowd was climbing the marble staircase now. She couldn't stay here on the attic stairs, reading recipes to herself. She folded the book around her lower arm and pulled her long shirt-sleeve right down, buttoning it tight at the wrist. She stuffed the last two blankets back into the box and closed the lid. She bounded up the last few steps to the top landing and hurtled from one narrow bedroom to the next, each with its white jug and basin on a stand. The floors up here were completely bare. No rugs or carpets to soften her footfalls.

'Servants' quarters!' she exclaimed.

What a life of luxury those sons of Morag and their families must have lived in this house, Eileen was thinking. Waited on hand and foot by an army of servants. That gold mine of theirs, if they really did own a gold mine, must certainly have been a rich one. But, oddly enough, the strong attraction that the house had held for her at first had now faded away. There was actually something about the place that she didn't like. Morag may well have visited her sons here from time to time but surely she hadn't ever felt at home in so much grandeur, so much pretentious display of wealth.

In the very last servant's bedroom at the far end of the

east wing, Eileen looked out of the window, abruptly remembering Malcolm. Far below, on the gravelled drive, she saw a sleek white car. A heavy boy sat in the front passenger seat, taking up more than his fair share of room. Someone a few years older, a young man rather than a boy, was hunched over the wheel beside him. He had black hair to his shoulders. His face, or the little she could see of it, was sharp and thin. And there were Malcolm and Jo, climbing into the back seat, laughing happily together, pushing at each other in playful fun. Malcolm seemed very sure of himself now. Talking so easily. Moving so confidently. Utterly different from that awkward, polite boy she had sat next to at lunch and the unbelievably rude boy who'd told her to push off. The door of the car below was slammed shut. Eileen saw it but did not hear it. She couldn't catch even a murmur of the engine's quiet hum as the car glided away over the gravel.

'Malcolm! Stop!' she shouted through the thick window-glass. 'There's danger!'

But no one heard her. The car sped smoothly towards the front of the house and out through the wide iron gates as she ran for the stairs. On her way down she met the inquisitive crowd surging up.

'What can we see, love?' a cheerful, plump woman asked her, pausing for breath by the stuffed lyrebird.

'Bedrooms!' Eileen answered promptly, her right hand gripping her left wrist to keep the recipe book safely in its place. 'Family bedrooms on the first floor, nurseries and schoolroom on the second floor, servants' rooms in the attic.'

'Amazing!' the woman murmured, shaking her head in disbelief as she plodded on upwards.

Back in the entrance hall, Eileen darted straight to the heavy front door. Eager people were pushing and shoving to come in as she was edging herself out. On the top of the steps she stood still for a minute, her eyes searching the sea of excited families that ebbed and flowed around the great house. Suddenly, one bright figure in the very heart of the crowd caught her eye. It was Chloë MacDonald from Allan's clan! But what on earth had possessed the girl? That nice, red-haired Chloë, who'd seemed so calm and serene only a few hours ago, was running in sheer panic through the hordes of relations, her arms waving wildly, her pale face taut with fear.

'Malkie! Malkie!' she was bellowing at the top of her voice. 'Malkie! Where are you?'

9

Bird in a Cage

Afterwards, Malcolm could not remember why on earth
he had agreed to get into that beautiful white car with Jo
and Andy. In retrospect it seemed like madness as well as
appallingly bad manners to have left the family gathering
without a word to anyone, but at the time it was the one
thing he wanted to do. Jo had assured him it was just for
a 'spin in Gem's new toy'. She'd introduced him to Gem
Craik, yet another cousin of hers she said, this time on
her mother's side. Malcolm noticed at once that Gem
looked nothing like Jo. His hair was smooth and long and
black, hanging right down to his shoulders, where hers
was so wonderfully pale and short. Gem was sitting proudly
in the driving seat of his Jaguar with Andy beside him.
Malcolm walked all around the car, admiring its lines,
touching its smooth paintwork lightly with his fingertips,
longing to feel its power.

'All right,' he said at last, smiling at Jo. 'Just for a quick
spin!'

'Good,' said Jo, pushing him gently in front of her as
she opened the door behind Andy's seat. 'Let's hop in the
back.' Andy turned his head to nod at them both.

As Malcolm leant back against the red leather
upholstery, Jo squeezed his hand. He felt extraordinarily

happy. The car moved almost silently over the gravel towards the gates. He looked out through the window with a sense of triumph, hoping to see someone he knew. Anyone would do. There was that Hick boy! What was his name again? David Hick. The boy who'd led him and Jo yesterday to hear his father reading Polly Hick's letter. Malcolm leant forward and waved enthusiastically. He desperately wanted to be seen. Seen in this car. Seen with Jo. David Hick stared back at him with blank eyes, startled for a second, but then, as he recognized Malcolm's smiling face and saw Jo beside him, he smiled in return and waved back. He certainly seemed to be impressed. Malcolm was content.

Once they were out on the open road, Gem Craik pressed his foot down hard on the accelerator. The Jaguar bounded forward. Malcolm loved the sensation of wild excitement as the trees flashed past in a blur of dark green leaves. Gem was overtaking every car in front of him. Effortlessly. Only fifteen glorious minutes later, as Gem swung the car southwards on to a highway clearly labelled 'To Melbourne', did Malcolm begin to feel uneasy.

'Jo!' he said, sitting bolt upright and letting go her hand. 'I think we'd better be turning back now.'

Jo laughed softly. 'We're not turning back,' she said. 'We're taking you to Melbourne. Just relax.'

'To Melbourne! But my uncle and aunt! Chloë! They won't know where I am. They'll be worried.'

'Bad luck,' Jo said.

'I only wanted to go for a spin, Jo! That's what you said we'd be doing! Why are you taking me to Melbourne? It's crazy.'

'Shut up, kid,' Andy barked, turning around from the front seat to glare at Malcolm.

Malcolm sank back and closed his eyes. He could not

quite believe this was happening. He felt as if he had strayed into a nightmare and he wished he could wake up. He opened his eyes again and looked at Jo. Her face was cold and hard.

In an instant Malcolm had leapt to his feet and thrust his arms forwards, one on each side of Gem's head. He clamped his fingers over Gem's eyes and pressed hard. Gem let out a shout and slammed on the brakes. The car skidded and lurched. Jo screamed. The car spun in a complete circle on the empty road and came to a stop with its nose under the trees. Everyone sat still, shocked into silence.

'You're a fool!' Andy roared at Malcolm. 'We could have all been killed! Jo, you come into my seat and I'll sit in the back with him. I'll tie him up so he can't move till we get there.'

White-faced, Jo did as she was told. Andy produced a length of yellow rope from one pocket, a thin leather strap from another. He bound Malcolm's ankles together, tied a firm knot and fixed the rope's end to his own leg. He pulled the strap tight around Malcolm's wrists and buckled it. Gem Craik, who had still not spoken a word, started the car again and edged it carefully back on to the road. He drove more slowly this time, glancing back at Malcolm now and then to make quite sure he was still sitting in his place. Malcolm closed his eyes. He could not bear to look at Jo's head any longer. He could not bear the pain of being awake.

'Queen Anne!' said Gem's laconic voice from the front seat. Malcolm woke up suddenly and remembered everything, his wrists and ankles chafing with the pull of rope and strap, his whole body aching. In the pocket of his jeans, the penny whistle stuck uncomfortably into his thigh. The Jaguar was parked in a quiet suburban avenue lined with trees. The gardens around every house were alive with brilliant flowers and whistling birds.

'Nice home our Aunty Daphne has here in Melbourne,' came Gem's voice again. 'Queen Anne.'

Malcolm stared at the house behind its low green fence and frowned in bewilderment. How could it possibly be Queen Anne? Queen Anne must have been dead and gone long before this city had been built. It was a handsome two-storey house in mellow red brick, with arched windows under steep gables and an elegant tower at the centre. A red door.

'The *style's* Queen Anne,' Gem explained with a laugh. 'Very fashionable these days. That house must be nearly a hundred years old. Our aunty's done really well for herself. Will I take him in, Andy, or will you?'

'I'll do it,' said Andy, undoing first the rope and then the strap. He gripped Malcolm's upper arm and pushed him roughly through the car's open door.

'No funny tricks now,' he hissed in Malcolm's ear, 'or I'll break your arm.'

Malcolm looked back at Jo. Her eyes were wide open but she paid no attention to him. She was staring straight in front of her and humming cheerfully to herself. Her arms were folded. There was no sign of that tartan sling.

'Shut up, Jo,' Andy roared at her. She stopped humming. Andy propelled Malcolm through the gate and up the neat pathway of white gravel between the rose bushes.

As they approached the red door it swung inwards as if by itself. A tall woman stood there, silent and unsmiling, a heavy grey cat in her arms.

'Hi, Aunty Daph,' Andy said to her. 'This is the boy. If he gives you any trouble, just ring me. It's only for the one night.'

The tall woman nodded. Andy let Malcolm's arm go and pushed him into the house.

'Did you tell him, Andy?' the woman asked, just as she was about to close the door.

'Not a word!' said Andy. 'That's your business, not mine. Jo and I agreed to bring him here, not tell him. We leave all that to you, Aunty.'

Andy swung on his heel and shuffled heavily back to the car. The woman shut the door. She looked carefully at Malcolm and he looked at her. He noticed her smooth dark hair streaked with grey, her elegant silk trousers and shirt, the gold sandals on her feet.

'So you're the boy!' she said at last. 'Malcolm Mac-Donald!' She seemed to turn every syllable of his name slowly on her tongue as if she were tasting it. 'Not a bad-looking boy really. A bit like your father.'

'You know my father?' Malcolm cried, full of new hope.

'All the Craiks know your father,' she said bitterly. 'Only too well.'

'Are you really Jo's aunt? Andy's aunt?'

'Not quite,' said the woman. 'They've always called me Aunty but I think that some remote kind of cousin would be nearer to it. Their mother was my second cousin. Or my third cousin. I forget exactly which. But Gem's my real nephew. His father is my brother. The Craiks are a very close family, however distant the connection. We never lose touch and we always help each other out. Now, come upstairs to your room. It's been ready and waiting for weeks.' And she gripped Malcolm's elbow and began to steer him up the carpeted stairs.

For weeks! Malcolm puzzled over the words. So she knew he was coming. But why? She was no real relation of his but only some remote cousin of Jo's and he was only some remote cousin of Jo's on the opposite side of the family. That wasn't any real connection. So why did she have a room all ready and waiting for him?

The bedroom at the back of the house was surprisingly soft. Warm colours in the bedspread and curtains. A thick woollen rug on the polished floor. Brightly coloured paperbacks in a low bookcase. A pair of striped pyjamas on the bed with towel and soap and toothbrush lying beside them. Malcolm glanced out of the window into the long sheltered garden with its three glossy lemon trees, the yellow fruit glowing like small moons among the shiny leaves. Beyond the lemon trees was a swimming pool, its waters clear and deep. Malcolm shivered. He turned back to face the aunt who was no aunt of his. Her gaze was stern and unblinking. A cold ribbon of fear ran up his spine.

'Why?' he demanded sharply.

'Andy should have told you himself,' said Aunty Daph, the grey cat still cradled in her arms. 'Andy or Jo. Sit on that bed and I'll break the news.'

Malcolm sat.

'You've heard of Charlie Craik, I suppose,' she said.

'Never!' said Malcolm. The woman looked surprised, even annoyed.

'Charlie Craik was my cousin,' she began slowly and deliberately. 'Not my first cousin. My cousin twice removed, as they used to say in the old days, but in our family we treat all our cousins as if they were our brothers and sisters. Your father,' she went on, 'is the man we hate. He was the crooked lawyer who was supposed to defend our Charlie against a charge of murder. Poor Charlie'd never committed any murder, of course. He was framed and the jury found him guilty. Your father failed us. He let the prosecution twist every shred of evidence against our Charlie. He let them brainwash that jury into their verdict. We paid your father good money to get our Charlie off the hook. He failed. Charlie Craik went to prison for life. He died in prison after twelve long years. *Your* father is the man who killed him.'

The woman was silent. Malcolm shivered. He was outraged by this caricature of his father but he had no idea what to say.

'Go on,' he said at last, trying to sound more confident than he felt.

'I will,' she said, lifting the cat to her shoulder and stroking its back in long rhythmic sweeps from neck to tail. 'Our family hounded your father right out of the country a year after Charlie had gone to jail. We rang his telephone number by night and day until he changed it. We put unspeakable packets into his letter-box till he moved house. We followed him to the new house and broke his windows. We lit fires by his back door. We arranged a car crash that didn't quite do the job we'd hoped it would do. No one ever caught us. The police suspected us, naturally, but they could never pin anything on to us. There are so many of us, you see. The police set a watch on your father's house so we got at his office in town. They set a guard on his office so we followed your mother to work. Not too close but close enough. She knew we were there all right. She rang the police but before they arrived with their pathetic sirens wailing we'd gone. In the end, your father had simply had enough. We'd broken his nerve. He left the country and he took your mother with him. We heard on the grapevine that he'd decided to give up the law altogether so we knew we'd won the battle. He'll never put any more innocent men into jail. We didn't bother to follow him to Scotland but we swore that if he ever came back to Australia, we'd deal with him in our own way. He hasn't come back but he's sent you in his place to this ridiculous MacDonald gathering. He thought we must've forgotten. The Craiks never forget a crime against the family and now our poor Charlie's dead it's time for revenge.'

'My father's not a criminal!' Malcolm protested, his voice angry but tears of fear in his eyes. 'And he's not a crooked lawyer either! He must have done his best for your cousin. I know what he's like. He's honest. He works hard. He did his best but he just lost the case. Lawyers can't win every case. They can't save everyone from prison.'

Aunty Daph made no reply.

'So what are you going to do with me now you've got me?' Malcolm demanded.

'That depends on how you behave. Things will go far worse for you if you try to leave this house before we're ready to move you on. The Craik network is all around you. Invisible but strong. Tomorrow we'll get you to telephone your father in Scotland. You can talk to him yourself. If he agrees to fly out here this week, we'll do you no harm. We'll just hold you safe till he comes. Sometimes in one house, sometimes in another. We'll keep you on the move. Once we've got him, we'll let you go. *He's* the one we want to hurt, not you. But, of course, if he *refuses* to come, then . . .' Her voice trailed away. The vagueness of this threat was somehow worse than something more definite.

'He'll never come!' Malcolm shouted defiantly, though he knew it was a lie.

'We think he will,' said Aunty Daph. Her eyes narrowed. She bent down to release the cat who ran straight towards Malcolm and began to rub against his legs, purring loudly. Without thinking, he bent to stroke the grey fur, to rub the soft ears, but suddenly he pulled back again.

You couldn't even trust a tom-cat in a place like this, he thought miserably.

'We'll eat at six,' said Aunty Daph and left the room. The door stood open.

Malcolm threw himself on to the bed. 'Jo! Jo!' he murmured in disbelief. 'How could you? I really liked you!'

He must have slept for an hour or more. When he woke the sun was setting in a fiery sky. The big cat was curled up at the foot of the bed. He stood at the window and stared down at the glowing lemon trees. He pulled Fiona's tin whistle out of his pocket and held it in his hands. There was something very comforting about that little whistle. Something simple and reliable. He put it to his lips and blew softly. He began to pick out the first tune that came into his head, a memory from childhood, an echo from a safer world.

> *Oranges and lemons,*
> *Say the bells of St Clement's.*
>
> *You owe me five farthings,*
> *Say the bells of St Martin's.*

A few notes to every verse. Every verse the same. It was easy. He played louder and with more confidence. The grey cat didn't like the noise. He jumped from the bed and ran howling from the room. Malcolm went on playing and playing till his fingers ached. If only someone could hear him!

Aunty Daph heard him only too well. 'Stop that racket, boy!' she shouted up the stairs. 'Come down and eat.'

He did not want to eat but he obeyed at once. His footsteps were silent on the carpeted steps.

'In here,' she called and he followed her voice into the dining room.

Aunty Daph sat waiting for him at the head of a long empty table. She pointed to the chair on her right. Malcolm sat. She served up rice and stew on to his plate. She nodded towards the salad bowl to tell him to help himself. He did. Mechanically he began to eat, not really tasting the food. He kept his eyes turned downwards. He did not want to look at this woman. Jo's distant cousin. There was something about her eyes that reminded him strangely of Jo. He did not want to remember how he had been taken in.

At the end of the meal, Malcolm went straight back to his bedroom, declining all offers of television, an evening swim in the pool or books to read. He shut the door. Night had come down quickly on the garden. No long Edinburgh twilight here. He got into bed, keeping on all his clothes apart from his shoes.

He slept at once, mainly to escape the fear and bewilderment that were gnawing at his stomach. He woke suddenly a few hours later, sitting up in bed and taking a minute or two to remember where he was. The room was flooded with moonlight. The luminous clock at the bedside showed two o'clock. If only he could find a telephone in this house, he thought in a sudden spurt of hope, he could ring Uncle Don. He knew the number off by heart. Dad had made sure of that. He crept to the door and opened it without any squeak of hinge or floorboard. He let one foot slide after the other across the carpet till his hand grasped the banister. Then silently, step by step, he moved down the staircase. The whole house was quiet. The suburbs were at peace.

In the hallway he paused for a second. He knew that the dining room lay to his left so he chose the door to his right. It stood slightly ajar so he had no need to turn any noisy handle. He pushed the door open. Enough light shone in through the wide window to show him heavy armchairs and a sofa, an upright piano, a desk. On the desk sat a white telephone. Tempted to run headlong across the room, he held back and then stepped forwards cautiously. His hand was on the receiver. He lifted it, tensing himself for the clink of a bell. None came. He held it close to his ear, pressing its coldness to his skin. The line was dead. He hunted for a plug that might have been pulled out of its socket but everything seemed to be in its right place. He put the receiver down again and picked it up again. Nothing but that same dead silence in his ear. He trembled.

Next he tried to open the window but it was locked with some kind of burglar-proof lock that needed a key. Back in the hall, he tried the front door but nothing responded to his searching fingers. That too was firmly locked and no convenient key was left there for him to turn. There was simply no way out of this house unless he tried to break a window. He climbed the stairs again, feeling far more frightened now as he went up than he had as he'd come down. He reached his own door and was startled by the sound of the aunt's voice, not far away. She was laughing softly to herself from a nearby bedroom. In her sleep perhaps? Or did she know exactly what he'd been doing?

At breakfast, in the same crumpled clothes that he'd slept in and without even bothering to wash his face or hands, Malcolm ate a slice of toast and drank the hot coffee but he did not look up. He kept thinking of breakfast at home in Edinburgh, high over the Meadows. The porridge. He couldn't stop remembering the porridge.

'We're moving you on today,' Aunty Daph said. 'You're going to Doll's place.'

'Who's Doll?' he demanded sharply.

'Another of poor Charlie's cousins.'

'I thought you said you'd let me speak to my father.'

'We've changed our minds about that. It might only cause trouble. He's sure to come of his own accord if we just wait. He'll know by now that you're missing. Your uncle will have told him.'

'Can't I ring my uncle? Just to tell him I'm all right. Though I'm *not* all right.'

Aunty Daphne shook her head.

'Rex Woodburn's sure to know where I am!' Malcolm said defiantly. 'He's part of your family! He'll know exactly where you're keeping me! He'll tell the police!'

'Rex is not really part of our family. He only married into it and his poor wife knew how to hold her tongue about our family affairs. He's never even met most of us. The Craiks like to keep to themselves. We don't trust outsiders.'

Gem and Jo came together with Andy to collect him in the middle of the morning. Malcolm was startled to see Jo again. He kept his eyes fixed on her face but she never once returned his puzzled, reproachful gaze. With Gem on one side of him and Andy on the other, each of them gripping an arm, he was led roughly to the gate. Aunty Daph stood in her doorway to watch him go.

This time there was no white Jaguar parked in the street. Jo and Gem and Andy had come in a shabby red van. They asked Malcolm politely enough to climb into the back. Andy followed him in and, turning on a powerful torch, he shut and locked the back doors. Then he tied Malcolm's wrists and his ankles to a heavy crate of apples. He sat down on the floor beside him. There was no window in the back of the van so the two of them sat in the dark. A thick metal wall cut them off from the two front seats so, from his prison in the back, Malcolm could not even see Jo's head. He felt desperately uncomfortable, leaning forward awkwardly, his whole body tethered by ankles and wrists. As the van bumped its way from one side of the great city to the other, he shouted out loud till his voice was hoarse.

'Help! Help!'

'Shut up!' Andy roared back at him every time.

But no one heard either of them over the roar of the traffic and the rattle of trams. Dad and Mum had always loved to talk about those trams. Now Malcolm could hear them but he couldn't see them. He was thankful that at least there was enough air to breathe but he couldn't see where it blew in. His prison had not even one chink of light.

The van stopped. Andy turned on the torch again so that he could untie Malcolm's ropes. He opened up the doors from the inside and pushed him out. Gem and Jo were waiting for him.

'Want an apple, son?' Gem asked him pleasantly as he grasped Malcolm's arm. 'Just help yourself before we leave the van.'

'No thanks,' Malcolm said, afraid that every innocent-looking apple in that crate might be poisoned, though he knew he was letting his imagination run wild with fear.

'Now listen to me, mate,' said Andy, jumping down from the van and grabbing Malcolm's other arm. 'We're taking you into Doll's place. Right? It's only a few steps. Gem'll stay on one side and I'll stay on the other. We'll be holding your arms like this until we've got you safely inside. Right? Jo'll walk in front. Any funny business and I'll knock you out. Right?'

Malcolm nodded.

Jo's face was completely expressionless as she led the

way. Andy and Gem steered Malcolm briskly over the pavement to a small brown house that was joined on both sides to the similar houses next door. The wicket fence was broken. The front door, its paint blistered and peeling, was just inside the gate. A curious festoon of white iron-work hung around the tiny veranda. Malcolm looked up in surprise at its pretty pattern of leaves and flowers. He saw dirty lace curtains at the one low window. He almost wished he could be back at the Queen Anne house with its cool tiled hallway and its soft grey cat.

Jo unlocked the front door with a big key of her own. She pushed the door open. Andy and Gem bundled him roughly inside and slammed the door behind them.

'Yoo-hoo!' Jo called out, as if to announce herself to someone within. Malcolm found it so strange to hear her voice again.

'Yoo-hoo!' he bellowed angrily, mocking her voice. He felt he had to make some kind of protest. Jo took no notice.

'Here I am, Jo,' came an old woman's faint call. 'In the usual place. Just walk through.'

Malcolm hated the smell of this house. It was musty and rank, a mixture of stale fried food and unwashed floors and something even more unpleasant, something unfamiliar. As they came to the door at the end of the passage, a terrible cry broke the air. 'Aaah! Aaah! Aaah!'

Jo laughed and opened the door. 'Your Chico's in a bad mood today, Doll,' she said in the fresh and kindly voice that Malcolm remembered so well.

The old lady sat on a sofa with a crocheted rug over her knees. Her white blouse was stained with tea and flecked with toast crumbs. Her hair hung down in grey wisps and strands. Her false teeth lay in a glass of water on the floor. Close beside her stood an enormous metal cage, stretching right up to the ceiling. Inside the cage a great bird with a crimson face was hanging upside down, clinging by its claws to a wooden perch, its long tail-feathers, red and yellow, swinging over its face. The bird's angry eye, half-hidden by the feathers, was fixed on Malcolm.

'Aaah!' shrieked the bird again and swung upright on its perch.

'Whatever is it?' gasped Malcolm in terror, pulling back at the door.

'Just my Chico, love,' said Doll with a gummy smile. 'Isn't he a beauty? Comes from Mexico. Don't ask me how I got hold of him, love. It's against the law but there's always a way.'

Malcolm shuddered. He felt a stab of pity for this magnificent creature of the forest who never should have been in a cage at all. Mad impossible ideas raced through his mind. Was this Doll going to put *him* in the cage with the bird? There was room enough. The whole place stank of bird. The floor of the cage was thick with droppings and old matted feathers.

'Aaah!' shrieked the bird, cocking his great scarlet head to look better at Malcolm.

'Sit down, love,' said Doll.

Malcolm stubbornly kept standing upright, fear rising in his mouth like bile.

'Hungry, love?' she asked him.

He shook his head. He looked at the woman. She certainly needed someone to look after her but it wasn't going to be him.

'Now, love,' she said, her voice cosy and friendly. 'I want to hear all about Scotland. I was there once, you know. Before the war. Walked right up Ben Nevis, I did.'

Malcolm didn't believe her. This woman could never have walked up Princes Street, let alone Ben Nevis, not even when she was young. If she ever had been young. Doll looked as if she'd been old all her life. She went on talking to him in her kind soft voice, calling him 'love' in that irritating way, as if she'd always known him. Perhaps, in a sense, she had.

'You look a bit like your father,' she said, scrutinizing his face. 'I saw him in court, you know. Poor Charlie Craik!' she went on. 'He was such a nice man.'

'Nice?' Malcolm shouted. 'He was a murderer!'

'Not a murderer, love. He just killed someone. Not the same thing at all. It was his duty really. He would've got off easy if your father had only done his job proper.'

'Killing's murder!' said Malcolm.

'Not always, love. What about soldiers killing the enemy? Do you call that murder?'

'Of course not! That's war!'

'Exactly what I mean, love. Poor Charlie was caught up in a war all right. Gang war, they called it. He was taking revenge. That's only natural. Duty, like I said.'

'It's against the law!'

'The law!' laughed Doll and shrugged her shoulders.

Andy was still standing guard, close by Malcolm's side, though he had let his arm go. Gem stood behind Doll's chair with one protective hand on her shoulder. Jo had settled herself into an armchair and was deep in a magazine she had picked up from the floor.

'Do shut up, Malcolm,' she said but did not look at him. 'Stop arguing!'

'But why?' he persisted in spite of Jo. He leant much closer to Doll. 'What's the point of it all?'

'Revenge,' said Doll, smiling benignly back at him. 'It's only natural, like I said. We want to give you a hard time, love. Your father gave our poor Charlie a hard time. We'll pay him back.'

'But Dad doesn't know a thing about this! You're not hurting him at all!'

'Oh, yes we are,' said Doll, her voice as gentle as ever. 'Daphne will have phoned him by now. From a public phone, of course. That's our new plan. She decided *you* mustn't talk to him but she'll just tell him that we're giving you a hard time for a few days. Not doing you any serious damage, love. Just giving you a hard time. That's enough to scare him. That's all we want. He's sure to jump on a plane and come out here himself. Then we can give *him* a hard time.'

Malcolm realized that this old woman was not quite as vague as she'd seemed to be.

Jo went on reading. Andy shifted about restlessly on his big feet. Doll drifted off to sleep, her old hands clutching at the rug, her toothless mouth hanging open. The great bird swung silently backwards and forwards in his cage, his bright eye fixed on Malcolm.

'Come on, Jo,' Gem said at last. 'We've got to get going.'

Without a word, Jo threw her magazine to the floor, stood up and left the room. Gem followed her. Andy was the last to leave. When the front door had banged behind them, Malcolm heard the sound of the big key turning in the lock. He sank down into the chair Jo had left empty. It was still warm. He stared at the swinging bird.

'Aaaah!' shrieked the bird.

Doll woke up with a start and looked at Malcolm with puzzled eyes. Then she remembered. 'There you are, love. We'll take good care of you. Me and Chico. Don't you be worried at all.'

10

Face to Face

'Chloë!' Eileen had called out the minute she caught sight of the red-haired girl running wildly through the crowd and shouting Malcolm's name in a kind of despair. 'Whatever's the matter?'

'It's Malcolm!' Chloë gasped out as soon as she was close enough. She spoke in a strange voice. Something between a sob and a whisper. 'One of those Hick boys told me he saw Malcolm going off in a white Jaguar a few minutes ago. I just can't believe it. Malcolm's such a well-behaved sort of boy. He'd never leave this gathering without saying a word to my mum or dad. So I've been searching for him everywhere in the orchard just to prove to David Hick that he must've *imagined* seeing him in a white Jaguar. But, Eileen, I can't find him anywhere in the grounds! Have you seen him in the big house? That's the only place I haven't looked.'

'I've seen him all right. But he wasn't in the house. I saw him from a high attic window. He *was* going off in a white Jaguar with two boys and that fair, skinny girl you told me about. Jo Woodburn. I met her for about two minutes at the end of the lunch in the orchard.'

'What did they look like?' Chloë demanded. 'Those two boys with Jo?'

'One of them was huge. He had spiky white hair like Jo's.'

'That's Andy. Her twin brother.'

'Jo's twin!' Eileen exclaimed in surprise. 'Apart from the hair, they're nothing alike.'

'I know. What did the other boy look like?'

'He was much older. Nineteen or twenty, I'd say. He was a man, really, not a boy. Very nice-looking. Black hair down to his shoulders. He was driving the Jaguar as if he owned it!'

'I don't know who that could be,' Chloë said puzzled. 'Were Jo and Andy *forcing* Malcolm into the car?'

'No, nothing like that. He seemed very pleased to be going with them. He and Jo were smiling and laughing all the time as they got into the back seat. Malcolm looked blissfully happy. But I felt worried all the same. I'd tried to warn him in the orchard but he just wouldn't listen.'

Chloë was astonished. 'Warn him of what?' she asked.

'That's the whole trouble,' Eileen admitted. 'I don't know. You'll think this is mad, Chloë, but I had, or I thought I had, a strange sort of meeting with Morag Mac-Rae. My ancestor, I mean. I know she's been dead since nineteen fourteen but I did think I saw her. She told me I had to warn Malcolm of some danger. She said I must stay close to him all the time. I've done my best but he wanted to go with Jo, not with me. There was nothing more I could do.'

'I don't think you're mad. Honestly, I believe you.'

'Thanks,' Eileen said, smiling at Chloë in relief.

'I was with Malcolm and Jo all day on Friday,' Chloë went on. 'It was uncanny. He seemed to fall more and more under Jo's spell. Or something like that.'

Eileen nodded. 'I saw it too,' she said. 'What can we do now?'

'Tell my parents first that he's gone,' Chloë said. 'Then tell them about your sense of danger. We needn't say that you met Morag. They'd think we're *both* mad! Then we'll find Rex Woodburn and see what he knows. He might guess who's driving that car and where they might be going.'

Chloë's parents were horrified. They agreed at once with Chloë that it was quite out of character for Malcolm to disappear like that without a word to anyone. They rushed to tell Rex who was relaxing at full length under the shady apple trees after his strenuous day. He refused to be the slightest bit anxious.

'You mustn't worry, Don,' he said genially to Chloë's dad, looking up at him from the grass. 'Malcolm'll be as safe as houses with my Andy and Jo. They're sure to look after him well. I don't know who that other lad could be. The one driving the car. Probably he's just some friend of Jo's. She's got so many friends. I don't know half of them.'

'But a friend with a *Jaguar*?' Eileen insisted. 'You must know him.'

Rex shook his head. He seemed sad all of a sudden. 'If my dear wife was still alive, she'd probably know. She kept up with Jo's life much better than I do.'

'We must phone the police,' said Chloë's dad.

'The police!' Rex gasped, sitting upright and grabbing his huge knees. 'It can't possibly be as serious as that!'

'I think it is,' Eileen said quietly.

'I think so too,' said Chloë's dad. 'I can't say too much, Rex, but Malcolm's father left this country sixteen years ago because he thought his life was in danger. We never believed him. We thought he was making a fuss about nothing but the plain fact is that he left. Now it's just possible that Malcolm might be in the very same danger.'

'Who from?' demanded Rex, his big florid face turning pale.

'People called Craik.'

Rex let out a roar of sudden understanding and heaved himself on to his feet. His broad, kind face seemed relieved rather than alarmed.

'The Craiks! That's my poor wife's family! She broke with them all after she married me, goodness knows why. I've never even met more than one or two of them. Very nice blokes, I thought they were. The Craik family is absolutely *huge*, I do know that. My poor wife used to say it was like an octopus but I simply couldn't understand what she meant. I think all families are wonderful, don't you? I'm sure we don't need to worry.'

'That's enough to go on!' Chloë's dad said tersely. 'I'll ring the police on our mobile in the car. Chloë, you and Eileen stand by the big gates to let us know if that white car comes back with Malcolm safe inside. I only hope it does!'

By the iron gates, Chloë took up her stand.

'Would you mind if I left you for a while?' Eileen asked her hesitantly. 'We don't really need two watching the gates, do we? There's another family problem I have to try to solve.'

'It can't possibly be as important as Malcolm going missing!' Chloë said, a sharp note in her voice.

'It is,' Eileen said with a smile. 'It's been going on since nineteen fourteen when Morag died.'

Chloë relented. 'OK!' she said.

What Eileen wanted more than anything else was a peaceful place where she could have a closer look at Morag's collection of bush recipes without being interrupted. She kept hoping that she might find some sort of clue in that thin black exercise book. She wandered behind the mansion to the long back garden, where a round glasshouse, crowded with pots of red begonias, stood in the centre of the lawn. The door was unlocked. She went in and sat on the only patch of sandy floor that was free of pots. She felt pretty sure that no one would see her there, surrounded by begonias, unless they came right up to the glass wall and peered in.

She undid the button at her wrist, took out the book and flattened it on her lap. She turned each page slowly, reading every single word of every recipe to be sure to miss nothing. Only near the very end of the book, where there were no more recipes but just a few blank pages, did she find anything odd. A whole page had been torn out. Eileen could easily see the jagged edge that was left. After two more turnings, an extra page had been roughly pasted into the book. A page with a jagged edge. Both sides of the extra page were covered with black writing but not the same kind of writing. On one side the hand was small and neat; on the other side it was large and untidy. She began with the untidy writing. There was a date at the top.

30 June 1914

On her last visit to us here, some months ago, our dear mother gave me her old recipe book just before she left. I was very surprised. I thought one of the girls should have it. But she told me to read the book carefully after her death and then to put it on the mantelpiece for my three brothers to read. I laughed. Why would grown men want to read recipes? But I kept it safe. Mother died last week. I faithfully read all the recipes one by one and very boring they were too. Near the end of the book I found the letter on the other side of this page. It was addressed to me and to my brothers. It made me very angry. I ripped it out in fury and I was about to throw it into the fire but something held me back. I remembered that our mother was a confused old woman who did not know what she was writing. I have decided not to put the book on the mantelpiece but to hide it in some safe place where no one in the family is ever likely to find it. I have carefully glued the torn page back into the book again. I am going to put it deep in the cedarwood box where our wives keep their cast-off blankets. No one ever opens that box. I could not quite bring myself to destroy my mother's words, though I wished I could. If anyone ever finds this book, I beg you, whoever you are, not to read her foolish letter. It was not meant for your eyes. Just throw the whole book in the fire. How I wish I could do it myself! Donald must leave that farm!

Duncan MacRae

Eileen hesitated but not for long. She knew she must turn the page and read Morag's letter. It was dated only a little over two months earlier than the first.

17 April 1914

My dear sons,

My time is near. This is my last visit and this letter is my last wish. I know you will honour it. I beg you to let my poor wee Donald keep the house and the farm where he has taken such good care of me in the years since your dear father passed away. Every one of you is wonderfully prosperous now and you have all been very generous to me. The four girls are comfortably settled. None of you needs the little farm or the old house. Please do not sell them off to strangers just to divide a pittance between you. Poor wee Donald has nothing in this world. He is not an easy man, I know. He has offended every one of you with his harsh tongue and his stubborn ways. But remember, my dear sons, he has suffered

*so much. His wife died when she was still young. He had
only one child where all of you have been blessed with many.
He was always poor but you are wealthy men. Remember
how he was always good to me, looking after me in the house
where I was once so happy with your father. I did not want
to leave that house. Poor wee Donald made it possible for me
to stay there. For my sake, dear sons, let him live out his
days in that house with its wee patch of fennel by the door.
Let him keep the farm. It is just enough land to support
him. Let him pass the house and the farm on to his son and
perhaps, one day, to a grandson. He will ask for nothing
more. Forgive him for his many angry words to you and to
your dear wives and children and to your sisters. Make your
peace with him and may God bless you all, my dear sons.*
    Your loving mother,
    Morag MacRae

Eileen read the letter a second time. As she reached the
end the first heavy drops of a sudden rain squall splashed
loudly on to the glass overhead. The squall blew quickly
into a torrential downpour, rattling and crashing the panes
all around her. She looked out on a white world. The
great house itself, the trees, the gardens – all were hidden
behind thick curtains of rain. She quite liked being alone
in this safe cave, imprisoned by the rain, unseen by anyone
and protected by the glasshouse roof, but at the same time
she desperately wanted to get back to the rest of Morag's
family, wherever they were, to show them this letter in
her hands. Both the letters.

She rolled the recipe book around her arm again and
fastened the button. She decided to make a dash through
the downpour to the front door on the far side of the
mansion. As soon as she took just the first cautious step
out of the glasshouse, her head was drenched. She bent

herself double to protect her arm and the book with her whole body. In that peculiar posture she began to run, slipping on the wet grass, feeling her shirt cling cold to her back, deafened by the steady roar of rain. She turned the corner to the front of the house and found she was not the only one running towards the steps and the great front door. She could make out other bent figures, shrieking figures, laughing figures, men, women and children from the family gathering, all dashing to find shelter from the storm.

There was room for everyone in that extraordinary house. The minute Eileen burst into the crowded hall, she heard Rex's voice again. That voice of his was everywhere. His efficient loudspeaker system seemed to reach into every cranny of the mansion.

'This won't last long, friends,' Rex was saying reassuringly. 'It's just a passing cloud-burst. Let's make the most of it and gather each of our family groups together again after this wonderful day. Allan's people can have the drawing rooms. He was the eldest after all. Morag's people can have the big entrance hall. If you can't all fit in there, the overflow can go up the stairs a little way or into the dining room. We won't ask anyone to go down as far as the kitchens. That's not really a comfortable place for sitting about. Kenny's family had better take the first floor where all the best bedrooms are. Please don't sit on the beds, whatever you do! Just use the chairs or the carpets but take off your muddy shoes first, please! The east and west passages are probably wide enough to take you all. Flora's lot can go up to the nurseries and the schoolroom. That would just suit our Flora! She was a wonderful teacher, as I might have mentioned before. And last but not least, Katie's family can go right up to the top floor. Plenty of corridor space up there even though the rooms are small.

That will give everyone a chance to dry out, exchange addresses, make plans to see each other again before too long. I'm sorry we've had to end in a rainstorm like this, my friends, but I think we've all enjoyed ourselves this weekend, haven't we?'

'Yes!' roared the happy, wet crowd.

'Three cheers for Rex Woodburn,' someone shouted from high up on the staircase. The cheers rang out. Rex murmured his embarrassed thanks through the microphone and everyone hurried upstairs or downstairs to be reunited with their right family group. Eileen was soaked to the skin. She pulled the book out from her sleeve. Only the shiny black cover was damp. The pages were dry. That was all that mattered.

She crossed the entrance hall to stand by the warm fire, wondering how she was ever going to break the news of Morag's last letter to all these people. She held the recipe book tight in one hand and seized her little white shell and the sprig of fennel in the other. Perhaps, somehow or other, Morag herself would find some way to help her. She would leave it to Morag. Gradually her soaked dress began to dry out in the heat from the fire. Her shivering legs were firm and still once more.

'Is there anyone here from Duncan's family?' Eileen called out loudly, not quite knowing where the words came from.

'Duncan came next to our Effie,' her mother called back to her from the far corner of the hall. 'He was Morag's eldest son.'

'We're over here!' came a voice from just inside the dining room.

Eileen ran towards them, jumping over the damp bodies on the carpet.

There were not so very many people in Duncan's

family. Eileen was surprised. She had imagined that a wealthy man like that Duncan would have had hundreds of prosperous descendants.

'I thought there'd be more of you,' she said to the first person in the group to smile up at her.

'We've all had our troubles,' he said.

'And most of us live in Queensland,' another man explained. 'All Duncan's children moved up there, you know. After the old man died.'

'It's too far for everyone to come,' said the first speaker. 'All that long way from Brisbane to Melbourne.'

'Well, I'm Eileen Gallagher. Effie was my ancestor, not Duncan, but we all belong to Morag. There are two letters I want to read to you. One's from Morag herself and the other's from your Duncan. Come closer! Come closer!'

Duncan's bewildered descendants bunched themselves close around Eileen. First she read them Duncan's letter, loud and clear but not so loud that her voice would carry too far out into the hall. Then she read Morag's letter. When she had finished, Duncan's family was utterly silent. They looked at each other in embarrassment, not knowing what to say.

'He was wrong!' one old man said at last. 'He never should've hidden Morag's letter like that. It was wicked!'

'I'm ashamed of him!' said a woman. 'I wish I belonged to someone else!'

'We had no idea!' said another.

'Whatever happened to poor wee Donald?' came a younger woman's voice. 'Are any of his family here today?'

Eileen nodded. 'Bob MacRae's his grandson,' she said, turning to face into the hall. 'Look, there he is with Gill, his wife. They're sitting all by themselves. Halfway up the first staircase. Just under the portrait of a bearded gentleman.'

'That bearded gentleman, as you call him, is our Duncan himself!' someone said with a laugh. 'And a fine figure of a man he is too!'

All the faces in Duncan's family turned upwards to look first at the splendid portrait of their ancestor and then at the wet and wizened old couple sitting at his feet.

'What can we do?' the younger woman asked. 'It's too late now. The harm's been done. Poor wee Donald's grandson must hate every one of us.'

'It's never too late!' Eileen insisted.

'Does he know about these letters?' asked the woman.

Eileen shook her head. 'I thought you should hear them first,' she said. 'That's only fair.'

'Let's go over and talk with that couple,' said the woman, getting to her feet. 'You come with us, Eileen Gallagher, and bring the letters. They must hear those letters. It's not going to be easy but we'll have to say we're sorry. Sorry for what our stubborn old Duncan did to their poor wee Donald.'

A murmur of agreement ran around Duncan's little group.

Eileen didn't know whether she was going to burst into tears of relief or shout for joy. She managed to do neither but calmly led all of Duncan's family across the hall, past Morag's other descendants in their happy, laughing circles, and up to the first turning in the marble stairs where Bob and Gill sat alone, wondering just what was going on. Nervously they got to their feet and faced the little crowd around them.

The young woman in Duncan's family took the letters from Eileen's hand. She introduced herself to Bob and Gill.

'I'm Marion MacRae,' she said simply. 'From Duncan MacRae's family. There's something we want to tell you.'

Then she read out the two old letters. No one in that hall could fail to hear every single word she spoke. The whole of Morag's great clan was listening in a stunned silence. Then the young woman held out her hand to Bob and Gill in turn. 'We're very sorry,' she said. 'All of Duncan's people are sorry. We want to set things right. Eileen says it's not too late.'

One by one, all the rest of Duncan's people came forward to crowd up the staircase to shake first Bob and then Gill by the hand. Bob and Gill murmured their bewildered thanks. Gill had a few tears running down her lined cheeks. Then a great cheer rose up from the rest of Morag's people.

Marion MacRae was offering all kinds of things to make up for Duncan's cruelty in selling off Morag's house and farm all those years ago and leaving poor wee Donald, rude and difficult Donald, without a roof over his head. Money, a house, a cruise, anything, she offered. But Bob shook his head and held up his hands.

'No, no! We don't want anything like that. Thanks all the same. But I know what we *would* like.'

'What?' chorused the listening crowd.

'We'd love to come up to Queensland next winter to see you all. Get away from Tassy's rain and cold. How about it?'

'You'll be very welcome!' said Marion MacRae and all the rest agreed, smiling in relief at Bob and Gill.

'What about the girl that brought us together?' said a voice from Duncan's family. 'She deserves a trip up to Queensland too! Eileen! That's her name! Where is she?'

Eileen stepped forward.

'How about your summer holidays?' Marion MacRae suggested, looking at Eileen. 'Come up for a really hot tropical Christmas and stay for five weeks! We'll pass you round like a wonderful parcel from one part of the family

138

to the next. If your mum and dad agree, of course.'

Eileen glanced down the stairs. Both her parents were beaming proudly up at her.

'Of course you can go to Queensland,' said Dad.

'Well done, Eileen!' called her mother.

'It was Morag who did it really,' Eileen protested.

'Three cheers for Morag!' called Bob MacRae in a flash. 'The best of the bunch!'

The heartfelt cheers rang out and filled the whole house.

Instinctively, Eileen put her hand deep into her pocket and barely touched a small white shell and a fading sprig of fennel. 'Thanks, Morag,' she said under her breath.

And at that moment, on the far edge of the laughing crowd that milled about in the hall, she thought she caught a glimpse of a dancing girl. An old-fashioned sort of a girl in a plain dark dress, her hair parted in the middle and pushed back behind her ears, a white scarf knotted around her neck. Eileen waved. The dancing figure waved back but then she was gone.

That was when Eileen remembered Malcolm.

11

Oranges and Lemons

Early on Monday morning, Eileen's father was taking down the three green tents. He was determined to have a few nights with his brother's family in Melbourne before they turned north to the Mallee farm again.

'The children need a radical change after all this Mac-Donald talk!' he said to Mum with a laugh, though he meant every word he was saying. 'It's time the Gallaghers had a look-in. Remember, the teachers said it would be all right if the kids took a couple more days off school.'

Mum agreed. In any case, it was years since she'd been in the big city. She loved it.

Eileen walked across the wet camping ground by herself to say goodbye to Bob and Gill. They were staying on there with their old caravan till the end of the week, planning the details of their trip to Queensland in the coming winter, talking over their extraordinary reconciliation with Duncan's family.

'We just don't know how to thank you, Eileen,' Bob said. 'We'd do anything for you!'

'There's only one thing I want,' Eileen said quickly.

'What is it?' asked Gill.

'Would you lend me Morag's necklace of emu feathers? Just for two days. Or three.'

'Why?' said Bob suspiciously, all his generous offers suddenly drying up.

'I need it. There's something more I have to do for Morag. The feathers will help me.'

Gill laughed, but her face was still kind. 'I don't see how feathers could help you, dear,' she said.

'I don't see it either,' said Eileen. 'But somehow I know it.'

There was a long pause.

'That necklace is very fragile,' Gill said. 'It might crumble away.'

'No, it won't. I'll take great care of it.'

'I thought you were going up to Melbourne for a few days,' Bob said.

'We are. It's in Melbourne that I'll need the necklace. I'm sure it is.'

'How would you get it safely back to us?' he persisted anxiously. 'I don't want you putting that precious heirloom of ours in the post. Anything could happen.'

'I wouldn't put it in the post. Dad's agreed to let us call in here early on Thursday morning on our way home so I can give it back to you. Geelong's right out of his way and he's not pleased at all but I persuaded him to make this roundabout journey in the end.'

Bob looked at Gill, his thick, grey eyebrows raised. Gill nodded. She went into the caravan and came out with the box in her hands.

'Here it is,' she said. 'Will you take the box too or do you want to wear Morag's necklace?'

'I'll wear it,' Eileen said making up her mind at once.

Gill draped the soft feathers around Eileen's neck, just inside the collar of her shirt. She tied a firm knot at the back.

'Now don't you go stepping under the shower with those feathers on, girl!' Bob said sternly. 'They'd be ruined! And keep well out of any rain!'

Eileen nodded. 'You can trust me,' she said. 'I'll keep the feathers safe. They'll keep me safe.'

Bob gave a short laugh. 'I would have thought you were talking absolute nonsense if I'd heard you say that a week ago, Eileen, but now I'm not so sure. Morag seems to have been doing some strange things in our family.'

'Whatever it is you have to do with that necklace,' Gill said with one arm around Eileen's shoulder, 'I hope it goes well. And we want you to come over to see us in Tassy in your September holiday week. Then we can tell you all about Queensland. Perhaps you'll come for a week every year. That's what Anna used to do. Every September.'

'I'd love to! Thanks!' And Eileen hugged each of them in turn.

The Gallaghers' last few camping things were loaded into their car. The last goodbyes were said. They drove off towards Melbourne with much cheerful waving and calling to Gill and Bob MacRae who stood holding hands in the middle of the camping ground.

'They're a funny old couple,' Dad remarked with a grin.

'I like them,' said Eileen, putting one finger inside her shirt to touch the feathers.

'So do I,' said Mum. 'The odd thing is that I feel I've known them for years.'

'Blood's thicker than water, that's why,' said Kev and laughed.

'We'll all have a welcome change of blood the minute we get to Melbourne!' said Dad briskly. 'Gallagher blood is a very different thing from MacDonald blood.'

'Not as different as all that, dear,' Mum laughed, giving his arm a squeeze.

Eileen's three Gallagher cousins in Melbourne were all much younger, much noisier and far more boisterous than anyone in her own family. Even the eldest boy was younger than Jack but with a much louder voice. For Eileen the afternoon slipped by in frantic activity – taking the little children to the swings and slides in the local park, reading them stories, helping them play on the floor with their train set, baking biscuits with them in the kitchen, attempting, unsuccessfully, to build a tree house with them in their back garden. She was thankful when the last meal of the day was over and the children were all in their pyjamas and ready for bed. Even then their demands had not stopped.

'Singing! Singing!' crowed the eldest.

'Sing what?' Eileen asked him, reeling with exhaustion.

'Anything! We'll help you!'

So she started on the old nursery rhymes, every one of them that she could still remember from her earliest years, making up her own tunes when she couldn't recall the right ones. 'Lavender's blue' came first and then 'Hey diddle diddle'. 'Pat-a-cake, pat-a-cake' was next and then 'Little Polly Flinders'. The children loudly demanded 'Wee Willie Winkie' followed by 'Little Jack Horner'. Kev suggested 'Humpty Dumpty' and 'London Bridge is falling down'. The children insisted on 'Old King Cole' and 'Sing a song of sixpence' and 'Baa, baa, black sheep'.

'That's all!' shouted Eileen at last, in weary desperation. 'I'm not singing any more. It's time for bed, you kids!'

'You forgetted de lemons,' said the youngest little cousin seriously.

Eileen was startled. 'What lemons?' she asked him, looking into his blue eyes.

' "Oranges and lemons",' he replied. 'Dat's my very best song.'

Eileen weakened. She couldn't resist his funny little voice. 'All right. And then you'll all hop straight into bed?'

The three heads nodded.

Kev and even Jack agreed to play. She and Kev made the bridge with their hands linked high in the air while Jack led the little ones underneath, marching one behind the other, all singing lustily. The four parents came to see what on earth was causing such a racket. Then they joined in too, bending low under the bridge as Eileen's clear voice led them all through the old familiar song.

> *Oranges and lemons,*
> *Say the bells of St Clements.*
>
> *You owe me five farthings,*
> *Say the bells of St Martins.*
>
> *When will you pay me?*
> *Say the bells of Old Bailey.*
>
> *When I grow rich,*
> *Say the bells of Shoreditch.*
>
> *When will that be?*
> *Say the bells of Stepney.*
>
> *I'm sure I don't know,*
> *Says the great bell at Bow.*

Here comes a candle to light you to bed,
Here comes a chopper to chop off your head.

Chop! Chop! Chop! Chop! Chop!

The children screamed in mock terror as the words suddenly changed from harmless church bells to something more sinister. Each one of them in turn was caught. Each one of them chose oranges or lemons and tagged on behind Eileen or Kev. Then the two teams pulled against each other until the lemons had finally vanquished the oranges with shrieks of laughter. Immediately Eileen carried the youngest to his cot and chased the other two into their beds. To her astonishment, they were asleep almost at once, quite worn out by all the excitement.

Later that night, in her own makeshift bed on the dining-room floor, Eileen kept singing that nursery rhyme over and over inside her head. She couldn't stop herself. It wouldn't leave her in peace. She felt for the emu feathers around her neck. They were warm and comforting but still the song ran on. Relentlessly. Obsessively. Like a mysterious spell that was holding her fast. Like a jumbled message she couldn't read. Like a secret code she couldn't crack.

Oranges and lemons,
Say the bells of St Clements.

And each time, as she reached the end, she felt a new shiver of fear at her neck.

Chop, chop, chop, chop, chop!

'Morag,' she said, speaking sternly into the darkness of the dining room, 'if you're trying to tell me something, you'll have to try harder. I don't know what you want me to do.'

And with that she fell asleep.

A heavy thumping on the front door woke Malcolm soon after six on Tuesday morning. The room was still dark. He pulled himself upright in the greasy armchair where he'd slept all night. Doll had offered him any one of several beds but they'd all looked far too disgusting, their sheets unwashed and grey. He'd chosen the chair instead.

The knocking grew louder, more insistent.

'What is it?' Malcolm gasped, bewildered by the din at the door that seemed to shake the whole house. He could hear the huge bird trembling in terror in his cage.

'Come on, Doll!' Gem's deep voice called impatiently. 'Open up! Jo's forgotten her key!'

'That'll just be Gem again, dear, with Andy and Jo,' Doll said calmly, turning on the light and shuffling a few paces into the room in her dowdy pink slippers and dressing-gown. 'They'll have the van all loaded up and waiting for you.'

'Loaded up with what?' Malcolm demanded but she made no answer as she shuffled out again and moved slowly up the passage to the front door.

'You took your time, Doll!' It was Gem's voice again. 'Isn't the boy ready?'

'Hurry up, Malcolm!' Jo's voice broke in on Gem's and echoed down the passage. She sounded harsher, sharper, colder.

Malcolm stood up. His clothes were crushed. He needed a wash and he needed food but he was desperate to get out of this house, no matter what came next. He almost ran to the front door, not even pausing to say goodbye to

Doll who stood there nodding her grey head and smiling toothlessly.

'Aaaah!' shrieked the bird behind him in a final mad farewell.

Jo was standing on the step between Andy and Gem. The faces of all three seemed very pale in the first streaks of daylight. Andy looked bigger and bulkier than ever, towering over the other two. Malcolm hardly glanced at Jo. He never wanted to look her in the eyes again. Gem's hair was smoothed back into a neat ponytail.

Andy took charge. He glared at Malcolm. 'We're taking you to Gem's stall at Victoria Market. Best market in the world.'

'And best stall in the market!' Gem broke in with a grin of pride.

'Shut up, Gem,' Andy continued. 'We're walking you to the van now. We want no trouble. Understand?'

Malcolm nodded. He'd do anything to get away from Doll and her bird. Anything to be out in the open where he could breathe.

The red van was waiting by the kerb. Andy climbed in through the back door to perch awkwardly on a crate of cauliflowers, his head almost touching the roof. As Malcolm peered inside he saw the whole space piled high with boxes. Boxes of fruit. Boxes of vegetables. Jo pushed him roughly from behind.

'I'll never fit in there!' he protested. 'Andy's taken the only place.'

'You're not goin' in there,' Gem barked. 'You're goin' in the front with me and Jo. We want to keep an eye on you.'

Malcolm was wedged between the two of them on the long front seat. He shrank away from both. His hands gripped his knees.

'You do look a bit of a mess, kid, if you don't mind

147

me sayin' so,' Gem said, glancing sideways at Malcolm. 'You'll have to clean yourself up before I let you come on me stall. When we've unloaded the stuff, I'll give you a basin of water and a lump of soap. The customers won't want to buy me goods from grubby paws like yours, will they? You'd put them off.'

Malcolm curled his fingers into his palms.

'Well, kid,' Gem said to him in a more friendly tone, 'who do you barrack for?'

'Barrack *for*? What do you mean?'

'The footy, of course. What else is there? What team do you support?'

'Hearts,' said Malcolm.

'Never heard of 'em,' said Gem.

'What about you?'

'Carlton, mate. Carlton every time. They're the greatest!'

'Never heard of them!' said Malcolm.

'Never heard of Carlton? Your dad hasn't brought you up proper.' Gem was quite indignant. 'He oughter phone through here to Melbourne every week to find out the scores. That's what most blokes do when they go overseas. They phone home every bloomin' week.'

'Not my dad!' said Malcolm.

Gem shook his head in puzzled disapproval. 'Tragic,' he said. 'Bloomin' tragic! No decent family values over there in England!'

'Scotland!' Malcolm snapped.

'Much the same!' said Gem.

'Not the same at all! Two different countries!'

Jo turned to stare at Malcolm in astonishment. 'You speak up for yourself much more than you used to,' she said but he made no answer. He didn't even allow himself to glance at her.

They were clearly getting nearer to the market now. The morning streets were crowded with vans and trucks, all laden with fruit and vegetables or other wares, all moving in the same direction.

'But *why* are you taking me to the market?' Malcolm asked, even wondering, in his maddest moments, if they were actually planning to *sell* him!

'That's where Andy and me comes every Tuesdee, mate. Most days we're here except Mondees. We have to keep an eye on you today so we thought we'd bring you to the market. You'll love it, mate. It's a great place.'

'And what's going to happen to me after the market?'

'That's not for us to decide,' said Gem. 'Andy and Jo and me, we just do what we're told. Someone else in the family'll be takin' over this afternoon. The family'll look after you. No need to worry.'

Malcolm shivered.

'Cold?' Jo asked him with a laugh.

'Here we are, mate!' Gem said. 'Victoria Market! Born and bred here I was, more or less. I bet you've never seen nothin' like it!'

Gem was right. Malcolm never had seen anything like it. The whole market was coming to life under a roof of corrugated iron held aloft by solid iron pillars. As Gem backed his van right up to his stall, Malcolm looked out through the window at the long rows of clothing stalls, bright with rolls of fabric, racks of shirts and skirts, piles of dresses and jeans. The sellers of fruit and vegetables were already busy along both sides of one wide aisle, unloading their vans and trucks, setting out their produce, hanging up their scales, writing out the new prices, tying on clean aprons, drinking mugs of tea, checking their money-boxes. As they worked, they called cheerful greetings to each other, glanced quizzically at the next stall's prices, stacked empty boxes under their trestle tables. Beyond all this good-humoured bustle and banter, the outer aisles were deserted, the empty stalls covered with hessian and canvas.

'I'd really like to bring you here on a Fridee or Saturdee,' Gem said as he jumped down from the van. 'Tuesdees are always a bit quiet like but on Fridees and Saturdees every single stall is open. Thousands of people walking up and down these aisles. Terrific noise. Great bargains. I love it. We make a packet on Saturdees. Muck in now, you three kids, and lend me a hand.'

Andy lifted the first heavy box from the back of the van. He staggered a few paces to the stall where Gem was already setting up his long trestle table and covering it with a huge green sheet of artificial grass.

'You and Jo bring those pears,' Andy said gruffly to Malcolm, nodding towards the next box in the van.

Malcolm did as he was told. There didn't seem to be much choice. As he moved mechanically backwards and forwards, helping to heave up each box and looking any-where but straight at Jo, he snuffed up the fresh scent of onions and carrots, celery and parsnip, oranges and lemons, pineapples and grapefruit, apples and pears, parsley and coriander, fennel and thyme. Gem unpacked his boxes one by one and set the fruit and vegetables out on the green-covered table in a fine display of colour. Even Malcolm could see that Gem's stall was the best in the row. A work of art.

Jo went off to buy doughnuts and coffee for them all. Malcolm scrubbed his hands clean under Gem's strict supervision, combed his hair and tied a fresh green apron over his clothes. Standing behind the stall, he wolfed down the sweet food and swallowed the drink that was so hot it scalded his throat. He was ravenous. He hadn't eaten a thing in Doll's house though she'd offered him plenty. The sight of it had turned his stomach.

'Can you add up, mate?' Gem asked him suddenly. 'In your head, I mean. Real quick. No pencil or paper. No calculators.'

'Of course I can,' said Malcolm.

'Right, then. I'll test you. My prices are clearly marked. Start adding now! Two kilos of those good red potatoes. One kilo of our best tomatoes. Three kilos of onions. Two caulis. Six grapefruit – the biggest ones. One and a half kilos of ripe bananas. One kilo of green beans. One pine-apple and a bunch of parsley. How much?'

'Fourteen dollars, thirty cents,' Malcolm said promptly.

'Right! You're on, mate! Never heard better in a kid your age. They must teach you *somethin'* over there in England, even if you don't know nothin' about the footy.'

'Scotland!' Malcolm murmured under his breath.

Jo had wandered off on her own to look at the clothing stalls. Evidently it was not her job to sell fruit and veg-etables but Gem and Andy stood ready and waiting. Mal-colm stood beside them as the first keen customers began to drift up the aisle with their trolleys and bags. Business was slow at first but then the shoppers came thick and fast. After a nod from Gem, Malcolm began to serve. All the stall-holders on both sides of the aisle were springing into life now, vying with each other, crying their wares in loud, singsong voices.

'Cheap caulis! Cheap caulis! Only one dollar today!'
'Oranges! Lovely navels! Ten a dollar! Ten a dollar!'
'Apples! Lady Williams! Buy a kilo! Buy a kilo!'
'Best bananas! Best bananas! Buy them here!'

Gem was bellowing louder than most, his deep voice echoing back from the roof overhead. He had a way with him all right. Malcolm began to like the man in spite of himself. It was hard to believe that Gem really had anything to do with the Craik family's revenge. Perhaps he was just being used.

'Here's the best bargains, ladies!' Gem cried. 'Lovely fresh celery going cheap today! Stop right here, mister! You'll never find better broccoli! Buy a kilo! Buy a kilo!'

Rather to his own surprise, Malcolm suddenly wanted to have a go himself at this calling and shouting. He tried out his voice, tentatively at first, but then louder and louder, really letting go as his confidence grew. Every cry felt to him like a call for help though there was no one to hear him except the crowds of shoppers and sellers in a busy market.

'Lovely lemons today!' he called. 'Cheap and juicy. Cheap and juicy! Oranges! Oranges! Don't miss a bargain! Buy a bunch of fennel! Buy a bunch of mint!'

Gem grinned his approval of Malcolm's strong voice.

At that moment, in full cry, Malcolm caught sight of a girl on the far side of the aisle. She was simply standing there, watching him and smiling. A girl about his own age with short fair hair, a few freckles, a nice smile, the family look! With a shock of recognition, he remembered her. She was surely that same girl he'd sat next to at the family meal in the orchard of the big house. When he'd wished he was with Jo. The girl he'd been so rude to. He couldn't even remember her name. Something Irish perhaps? Colleen? Maureen? Kathleen? What was it?

The girl was walking slowly towards him. She was taking a fat purse from her pocket. She was ready to buy.

'Can I help you, miss?' he asked her politely, not quite sure if people ever did say 'miss' in Australia.

'Two large oranges, please,' she said quietly. He could hardly hear her.

'Only two, miss? That's not many! Ten a dollar, miss! Make a day of it!'

The girl shook her head and smiled again, stretching out her hand to take the oranges. 'And two lemons,' she said. This time she leant closer to him as she took the fruit. 'Malcolm?' she whispered.

He nodded. He wanted to keep this girl there. He didn't want her to leave. He prattled on quickly. 'How about some lovely apples, miss? Only one dollar sixty a kilo!'

'No thanks. Any fennel?'

'Wonderful fennel, miss. Look here it is! Just smell it!' and he pushed a great handful of the stuff close to her nose.

'Just half a kilo, thanks.'

The girl took the fennel and held it in front of her face. With one cautious eye on Gem and Andy who were busy with other customers, she talked to him from behind the green feathery leaves so no one could see her lips moving.

'Malcolm! When I wreck this stall, be ready to jump over the counter and run with me as fast as you can. Mum's waiting outside in a taxi!'

'Wreck the stall!' he muttered in alarm, picking out a few apples and weighing them up in the scales though she had never asked for them.

'Yes, I'll take those apples, thanks,' she said out loud. 'That'll be all for today. How much?'

'Two dollars, thirty cents,' he said, passing her the apples and still wondering what she meant by 'wreck'.

The girl gave him the exact money and set her shopping bag carefully on the ground. She pushed her purse into one large pocket of her loose jacket and the whole bunch of fennel into the other. With two strong hands she grasped the edge of the green grassy sheet where it hung down in front of the table. She took a deep breath, leant back and pulled hard with a sudden, desperate force.

In an instant there was utter chaos on Gem's stall. The lovely pyramids of fruit collapsed. Cabbages, parsnips and bunches of bananas tumbled to the ground. Golden lemons were pitched this way and that. Oranges rolled over the pavement. Carrots flew through the air.

'Quick!' the girl cried in triumph. 'Jump, Malcolm, jump!'

He vaulted straight over the counter. The girl grabbed his hand and ran.

'Your bag!' he panted. 'You left it behind!'

'No worries!' she laughed. 'Run, Malcolm, run!'

Behind them, Gem was bellowing in fury. Stall-holders and customers were rushing to pick up the tumbling fruit, to help him set things to rights again. In their eagerness to rescue his produce, the good Samaritans had blocked up the whole aisle. Gem and Andy were pinned behind their stall.

'Stop them!' Gem cried out in helpless despair, both arms waving, as Andy turned to scramble over the empty boxes to get out at the back of the stall. But Malcolm and the girl were well away. Down past the other stalls of fruit and vegetables, over a small road, past the meat and the fish, a swing to the right past the cakes, the cheeses, the garlic sausages strung up high, a swing to the left past the breads, the croissants, the chickens. And there, out in the wide Melbourne street, a taxi was waiting with the engine running. A smiling woman on the back seat was pushing the door open towards them.

'Quick!' said the girl. 'Jump in!'

Malcolm jumped and the girl followed. The taxi drove off at once. Malcolm and the girl sank back, gasping for breath.

'Sorry, I've forgotten your name,' he said honestly, looking her straight in the eyes. 'But I remember your face.'

'I'm Eileen Gallagher,' she said with a smile. 'And this is my mum.'

'How did you know where to find me?' he asked her, still stunned with surprise.

'Morag told me.'

'Who?'

'One of the ancestors. Morag MacDonald from the Isle of Skye. She married Rory MacRae.'

Malcolm laughed out loud. 'But, Eileen,' he protested. 'That old Morag's dead and gone. How could she possibly tell you?'

'It's a mystery,' Eileen said slowly, her fingers inside the neck of her shirt again, stroking the emu feathers. 'Morag may be dead but she's not quite gone. I've seen her, Malcolm. I've heard her voice.'

'And she *told* you to go to Victoria Market?'

'Not quite like that. She hinted. Through the scent of fennel and a necklace of feathers. Through an old song, a nursery rhyme. "Oranges and lemons." When I told Mum this morning that the rhyme kept going on and on inside my head, *she* was the one who suddenly understood it. It was Mum who actually said, "We'll go to Victoria Market. That's the best place."'

'But when you got there, how on earth did you find me? I could have been anywhere.'

'I made for the fruit stalls first and then I heard you! That strong Scottish voice of yours filling the air with your cries about oranges and lemons. And then, at last, I saw you. I remembered your face. Morag did all the rest.'

This time Malcolm didn't laugh. 'It's the second sight, Eileen!' he said in admiration.

155

Eileen nodded. 'That's what Mum thinks too,' she said.
'You're the one with the gift,' said Malcolm.

Eileen's mother smiled at them both. And as the taxi whirled them through the sunny suburban streets of Melbourne, all three of them became more and more aware of the powerful scent of fennel. Suddenly remembering where she had put it, Eileen pulled the green bunch from her pocket and flourished it over her head.

'Good old Morag!' she cried out loud and the taxi driver looked round in surprise at these three strange passengers in the back of his sober cab.

12

Finding a Voice

The Gallaghers' house was noisy with the racket of children. Eileen led Malcolm to the one quiet room and a
telephone. He dialled his uncle's number in Geelong and
she left him alone.

'Uncle Don?' he said.

'Malcolm! Are you all right? Where on earth are you?'

'I'm somewhere in Melbourne with Eileen Gallagher's
family. She got me away from the Craiks. She rescued
me.'

'Your father's just been on the phone again, Malcolm.
He's in a terrible state! Ever since I had to tell him you'd
disappeared. Now he's trying to get a seat on a plane. He
wants to fly straight out here.'

'Stop him, Uncle Don! Stop him from coming! I'm
perfectly safe with the Gallagher family. Dad mustn't
come! Just tell him to remember Charlie Craik!'

'But Charlie Craik's dead, Malcolm. He died in prison.
He can't hurt your father.'

'He's dead all right, but he still lives on in his family.
Jo Woodburn's connected to the Craik family. You must
know that by now. She's connected through her mother,
not her father. She's got a huge network of Craik cousins.
They're just like the MacDonalds!'

'The Craiks are *nothing* like our MacDonalds!' Uncle Don shouted indignantly into the phone. 'They're a bunch of criminals! Everyone knows that!'

'But they've got the same family feeling. They think they're the best family in the world. They'd do anything to help each other.'

'What exactly were they trying to do to *you*, Malcolm? Tell me the truth!'

'They just wanted to scare me and to keep me hidden. They did it pretty well too. I *was* scared. Terribly scared, as a matter of fact. But their real aim was to get Dad back to Melbourne. They were sure he'd soon come searching for me. It's Dad they really wanted, not me. That's why he mustn't come. Uncle Don, they could *kill* him!'

'*Kill!* I'd better talk to the police again. Where do these Craiks live?'

'I don't know. I was in two different houses but I've got no idea where they were. The only definite thing I know is that Gem Craik has a stall in the market.'

'What market?' Uncle Don cried in alarm. 'The black market? The drugs market?'

'No, no. Just Victoria Market. That's where Eileen found me. Because of the oranges and lemons.'

'Oranges and lemons? Malcolm, I really don't know what you're talking about. You must still be in a state of shock. I'll drive up to Melbourne this minute and get you if you'll just tell me where you are.'

'No, there's no need. Eileen says her family will bring me back to you this afternoon. They were going to leave here tomorrow anyway and they don't mind setting off today. *Please*, Uncle Don, just ring Dad this minute and tell him not to come. That's the only thing that matters.'

'All right. But the police are bound to want to talk to you.'

'I'll talk to them. The police can see me in Geelong tonight or tomorrow. I'll tell them all I know.'

Uncle Don seemed satisfied at last. He hung up. Malcolm sat there, still a little dazed. Eileen put her head in through the door.

'Is everything all right?' she asked.

Malcolm nodded. 'I think I'm in time to stop Dad flying out here but Uncle Don's nearly out of his mind with worry. I felt a fool not knowing where I am. Where exactly am I?'

Eileen laughed. 'You're in Kew. I'll write down this address and the phone number in case you ever need them.'

When everything was settled, Malcolm had a shower. He wished he could have clean clothes too but at least the hot water pouring over his body made him feel much better. He sat down with the two Gallagher families for a rather boisterous lunch until, at last, Eileen's father was ready to set off for Geelong. Malcolm travelled in the back seat with Kev and Eileen and Jack all crammed in beside him. He fell asleep on the journey.

At Uncle Don's house the welcome was ecstatic. Aunty Jan hugged and kissed everyone in the Gallagher family, even Eileen's dad who looked surprised but pleased. Chloë was crazy with delight, laughing half of the time but then suddenly bursting into tears when Malcolm had told his story.

'So they didn't actually bundle you into that Jaguar in the first place, Malcolm,' Aunty Jan said to him, still puzzled. 'They didn't force you. You went with them of your own accord.'

Malcolm nodded.

'But why?' she asked him.

'It was Jo Woodburn,' he admitted, embarrassed to be asked so directly for an answer. 'I wanted to go wherever

159

she was going. I really liked her. I thought she liked me. I was taken in.'

'It could have happened to anyone, dear,' Eileen's mother said to him, one hand on his arm. 'And you'll never make the same mistake again.'

'I'll tell you something else, Mal,' Kev broke in with a laugh. 'It'll make a jolly good talk for your school when you get back home.'

As Malcolm grasped what Kev was saying, a wonderful new idea came into his head. 'Aunty Jan, would you let me phone Edinburgh? No, not Mum and Dad. I just have to speak to a friend. I'll be really quick.'

'But it's the middle of the night over there!' Uncle Don protested. 'Or three in the morning, anyway!'

'That doesn't matter. She won't mind.'

'Who?' demanded Chloë, her green eyes alert again, but Malcolm didn't reply.

'Of course you can use the phone, dear,' Aunty Jan said calmly. 'Come into the next room where you'll have some peace and quiet. Take as long as you like.'

Malcolm dialled the number.

'Fiona?' he said, recognizing her voice at once and glad she'd been the one to answer.

'Malcolm!' she gasped. 'Are you all right? Your dad's been frantic about you but he wouldn't tell us anything. I thought . . . I thought I'd never see you again!'

Fiona's voice was shaking. Malcolm broke in on her confusion.

'I'm fine. Yes, honestly. And I've got so much to tell you when I come home. Fiona, there's something I want you to do for me.'

'Of course. What is it?'

'I'd like you to speak to Mr Murray for me. Ask him if I can give a talk in the English class next week.'

160

'*You?* Give a *talk*? How long will it last? Three minutes?'

'No, no, Fiona!' Malcolm laughed. 'It'll last about forty minutes. Maybe an hour. I've got so much to say, you see. I'll need a lot of time. Be sure to ask him.'

'I'll ask him all right! And I'll tell everyone at school that you've gone a bit crazy!'

'No, I haven't. Fiona, that tin whistle you gave me! It really helped me.'

'Helped you? How?'

'I'll tell you when I see you. We'll be talking for days and days. Just the two of us. I really missed you, Fiona.'

'I missed you too. I was afraid you might find some wonderful new friend out there. Some cousin you liked much better than me.'

'Never!' breathed Malcolm, hot tears in his eyes.

'And guess what your dad said yesterday!' Fiona rattled on. 'He said he never should have tried to talk you into doing law! He says of *course* you can be a vet if you want to. He says you'll be the best vet in the whole of Scotland!'

'Brilliant!' Malcolm shouted. 'See you on Sunday! Fiona, I love you!'

At the end of the afternoon, as the Gallagher family drove off towards the camping ground at Ocean Grove, they waved out of the windows of the car until they could see Malcolm no longer. Bob and Gill were delighted to welcome them back sooner than expected. Eileen took off the emu feathers from around her neck for the last time and settled them safely back into their box again.

'They really helped me,' she said simply. There was a pause. 'We're going to camp here tonight,' Eileen went on, 'and we'll set off at five in the morning. Dad says it's too late to start for home tonight.'

'He's right,' said Bob. 'An early start is always the best. So let's all eat together tonight, Eileen! I caught a whole bucketful of fish today. This won't just be a meal! It'll be a feast!'

When the feast was over, Eileen fell asleep in her own little tent while a huge yellow moon shone down on the camping ground. And far away, near Mount Macedon, the same yellow moon was shining down on a derelict chimney and a patch of fennel. The old woman was still wide awake. An old woman with a brown straw hat on her silvery hair. An old woman with dark eyes and a smiling face. She wandered happily up and down among the fennel bushes, gathering a bunch of the feathery leaves into her arms. Her voice filled the night with a song from her childhood. A song from the Isle of Skye.

May the angels be with us wherever we go,
Over the green hills and over the sea,
Watching and keeping us, far from our home,
Over the green hills and over the sea.